THE *fix* UP
FIRST IMPRESSIONS

TAWNA FENSKE

Entangled Publishing, LLC
2614 South Timberline Road
Suite 109
Fort Collins, CO 80525
Visit our website at www.entangledpublishing.com.

Lovestruck is an imprint of Entangled Publishing, LLC.

Edited by Stephen Morgan
Cover design by Heather Howland
Cover art from iStock

Manufactured in the United States of America

First Edition December 2015

To the talented and dedicated marketing and PR crew I work with at my day job (you know who you are!) Thanks for making this crazy dual-career life possible for me. You guys are the best!

Chapter One

"As you can see, this is impressively sturdy."

The saleswoman smiled at Ben, then turned and presented her backside. Or the hand-carved headboard. Really, it was tough to tell what she was presenting as she leaned across the mattress in a short gray skirt.

Ben wasn't sure where to direct his gaze, so he settled for looking around the furniture warehouse at endless rows of tables and armoires and bookshelves. This whole shopping trip was baffling. He was exhausted and jet-lagged and not entirely sure what was going on. He'd been in this store less than ten minutes, and already the saleswoman had touched his arm a dozen times.

Normally, a woman being so aggressive might be a welcome surprise for Ben, but this one just didn't do it for him. Not that she seemed to notice. She subtly raised her backside a little higher for his viewing pleasure.

"You see that?" she said. "That's quality craftsmanship."

"Er, yes. Indeed."

She gripped the slats of the headboard with both hands

and gave it a firm shake.

"Notice the sturdiness?" she asked, turning to peer at him over her shoulder. "No jiggling at all. That's solid wood."

"Er, yes." Ben took a step back and folded his hands behind his back. "No jiggling. Oak, is it?"

He swallowed and glanced around, trying to look anywhere but at the pert posterior wiggling in the air. Now wasn't the time to get distracted. He had a lot of work to do, and none of it involved staring at a sales clerk's rear end. It was his first week on the job as CEO of Langley Enterprises, and his father had handed him a corporate credit card and instructions to purchase new furniture for Ben's new "primo office" and "primo penthouse." His dad's words, not his. His father's only requirement for what furniture to buy was "none of that bachelor pad shit you usually get."

So here he was, doing his best to look like a refined CEO, instead of like a geeky engineer trying not to notice the saleswoman's ass waving like a flag in front of him. She turned and slithered off the bed, reaching out to touch his arm again.

"You see anything you like so far?"

"Uh, yes," Ben said, nodding. "That credenza over there is very nice."

She frowned, then followed the direction he pointed. "Of course. That's one of our newest models. Would you like to take a closer look?"

"Sure," Ben said.

She turned with a dramatic pivot and began to strut in that direction. He followed, stooping down a little as he ducked past a froofy canopy covering a king-sized bed. At six-foot-three, he was accustomed to slouching to avoid hitting his head or intimidating people who expected a guy with a PhD in engineering to be a scrawny pencil pusher with glasses.

You've got the glasses, he told himself, shoving them up his nose as he followed the saleswoman across the floor. He stepped past a slender brunette standing on the other side of the bed studying the tags on a pillow.

"Pardon me," he said.

The woman glanced up as he passed and reached up to tuck a strand of sleek, espresso-colored hair behind one ear. Her eyes were a remarkable shade of violet-gray, and she flashed him a smile he could have sworn seemed sympathetic.

He gave a small shrug in return—*if only you could help me*—but then the moment was over as the saleswoman grabbed his arm and towed him to the front of the credenza.

"As you can see, this piece is manufactured to the highest quality standards with French dovetailing, adjustable glass shelves, and a one-of-a-kind, patented touch-lighting system that's unique to this design."

"I know," Ben said, stroking a hand over the surface. "I hold the patent."

"I beg your pardon?"

"I developed that lighting system. I engineered specialized thermoplastics using phenolic resins crosslinked with fiberglass aramids to produce a unique design that—"

He stopped talking, realizing the saleswoman's eyes had gone surprisingly wide. He felt a faint swell of pride at the thought she might be admiring his workmanship, then realized she was staring at his left hand.

What the hell? He didn't have any scrapes or bruises or rings or tattoos or anything besides five fingers and a palm.

"That's incredibly interesting," she cooed. "Maybe we could get together later and you could tell me all about—"

"There you are!"

He turned to see the woman with the sleek black hair striding toward him. She wore a broad smile and a sparkly ring on the hand that reached out to slide around his waist. Before he could say a word, she snuggled up close to him and extended a handshake to the saleswoman.

"Thank you so much for taking care of my husband while I was busy over there," she said, giving the saleswoman's hand a hearty shake. "He's a little clueless when it comes to furniture, I'm afraid."

Ben blinked down at her. *Husband?*

"Er, your husband?" The saleswoman took a step back, casting a nervous look at the woman with the strangely beautiful eyes.

"Yep! We've been married for—gosh, almost five years now, honey?"

The saleswoman glanced at Ben's hand again, and he understood what she'd been looking for. A ring. Which he didn't have.

Fortunately, his patron saint was well ahead of the saleswoman.

"His ring's at the jeweler having a little repair work done, but the bonds of matrimony are stronger than gold. Isn't that right, baby?" The brunette cuddled tighter against him, and Ben found himself instinctively putting an arm around her. She felt nice there. Warm and soft and—

"Of course," Ben agreed. "Uh, sweetie—weren't you saying you wanted to check out some of the items from the new catalog?"

"Absolutely! Their fall line is always so spectacular." She smiled up at him like he'd offered her diamond earrings wrapped in bacon, and he wondered what she was wearing under that silky black top.

"I'm sorry, will you excuse me a moment?" the saleswoman said, taking another step back as she folded her hands together. "I need to—uh—check something."

"No problem," Ben's fake wife said, beaming up at him. "We'll be right here talking about where this will fit in our living room."

"Er, right."

The saleswoman turned and scurried away, leaving Ben to stare down at the wife now affixed to his arm. She tucked a loose strand of hair behind her ear and glanced in the direction the saleswoman had retreated.

"I hope I read that right." The brunette scooted out from under his arm, and he instantly missed her softness. She looked up at him with those odd violet-gray eyes and smiled. "You looked like you were being eaten alive there, but too polite to tell her to back off."

"Eaten alive," he repeated, a little mesmerized by the woman's eyes. "I'm not entirely sure."

"Seemed like that's what was going on. Salesgirl sees a big guy with a big budget and big—" She paused, then gave a small shrug. "Well, sometimes it brings out the worst in women."

"Thank you," he said, meaning it. "I've been flying back and forth between cities all week, so I'm a little jet-lagged and distracted. I guess I wasn't even a hundred percent sure I was being—uh—"

"Hit on? Ogled? Mentally undressed?"

"Right." He cleared his throat. "Not until you pointed it out. Thanks for the rescue."

"No problem. Pay it forward sometime."

"Is that real? It's huge."

She blinked, then glanced down at the paperweight-sized rock adorning her ring finger. "Nah, I keep it in my purse for when I want to avoid getting hit on at ladies' night."

"Does it work?"

"Not with the real jackasses, which probably defeats the purpose, huh?"

He nodded, not sure what to say to that. "I'm sorry, what was your name again?"

"Holly. Holly Colvin. I'm the owner of First Impressions."

"First Impressions?"

"We're a public relations and branding firm that specializes in creating and remaking corporate identities." She fished into her purse to pull out a business card. She held it out to him and Ben started to reach for it, but Holly withdrew her hand.

"Shit. Vampira the Sales Queen is headed back here."

Before he could say anything, Holly was sliding her hand around to cup his ass. For a few beats, he thought she was copping a feel, and he hoped like hell she kept doing it. Then he realized she was tucking her card into his back pocket. She grinned and tilted her head back to look up at him.

"Gotta commit to the role, right?"

"Right," he murmured, staring down into those slate-speckled eyes. "We certainly do."

"I suppose we could throw in a little something extra if you really want her to buy it."

"Like what?"

Her lips parted slightly, almost like she was braced for a kiss. Or was that his imagination? It seemed hot in here, and he was getting dizzy, and now all he could think about was claiming those perfect lips.

"I'm sure you'll come up with something," she murmured.

Her mouth looked so soft, so inviting, and he could have sworn her lashes fluttered low the way they might if she were waiting for him to make a move. A *big* move.

He knew what he needed to do. What he *wanted* to do.

And with that, he bent and kissed her.

•••

Holy mother of hard-ons.

Okay, Holly couldn't actually detect a hard-on, but she was feeling every other inch of this luscious man with the enormous hands and the sexy-geek vibe and the magical mouth that was kissing her silly in the middle of the damn furniture store.

Had she started it, or had he? Did it matter?

"Ahem."

She pulled back, dizzy and breathless. She turned to see the saleswoman standing a few feet away with her arms crossed and an expression that suggested Holly was close to getting kicked out of the store. Fine by her. This place gave her the creeps. Everything was ridiculously expensive and high-polished. Furniture aside, what kind of store let its employees blatantly hit on customers who were either too polite or too clueless to beat them away with a stick?

Can't say I blame her, Holly mused, looking up at the towering figure beside her, whose tortoiseshell glasses brought out the amber flecks in his brown eyes. His shoulders were broad and muscular beneath a dress shirt that looked expensive, outdated, and in need of some serious ironing.

Who the hell is this guy?

Holly tucked her hair behind her ear and smiled at the saleswoman. "Sorry about that. Credenzas get me hot."

Her fake husband nodded. "I think I'll take one for my office. Well, one for my office at the Langley headquarters, and one for my home office. So that would be two." He cleared his throat and glanced at Holly. "Two credenzas."

"You said you own Langley Enterprises?" the saleswoman asked, and Holly blinked in surprise. Magic Hands here owned the largest manufacturing firm in the country?

"No, not the owner," he said. "I'm the new CEO. I've been on the engineering side of things for the last decade, but my father's looking to step away from domestic management and into international relations, and anyway—" He shrugged. "Here I am."

"Here you are," the saleswoman agreed, looking decidedly less pleased about that than she had before Holly stepped in. "With orders to fill up a whole penthouse and an office. Here, I brought you a few catalogs with some of the newest items that aren't on our sales floor yet."

She thrust the glossy pages at them, and the guy reached out to take them with a nod. "Thanks. I'll take a look."

"Wonderful," the saleswoman said. "I'll leave you two alone to browse. If you need anything, I'll be right over there."

"Thank you," Holly said. "It's been a pleasure."

"Likewise."

The saleswoman turned and flounced away, leaving Holly alone with the guy whose handprints were probably still on her butt. She turned to look at him and saw his warm brown eyes were studying her with an odd mix of curiosity and intrigue.

"Thanks again," he said, holding up the catalogs. "This is how I'd prefer to shop anyway. This, or online."

"Not one for the in-person contact?"

He gave a funny snort and shook his head. "As my father would be the first to tell you, I'd sooner gnaw off my own foot than deal with people."

"And you're a CEO?"

He shrugged. "I am now, but I spent the last decade in the trenches of the company doing product development. This is—uh, new territory for me."

"You don't say." She bit her lip, hoping she hadn't sounded too judgmental. "Well, look, I have to run. I just came in to look for some new pillows on my lunch break, but I had no idea there were this many to choose from. Antimicrobial buckwheat? Spine alignment memory foam? Who the hell comes up with this stuff?"

"Probably those marketing and branding types," he said, giving her a small smile that left her tingling all the way down to her kneecaps.

She smiled back, wondering if anyone had ever told him he ought to smile more. It did wonders for his features, which weren't bad to start with. He could use a haircut, maybe, and a shirt that was a bit more tailored for those impressive biceps, and maybe—

"It was lovely meeting you, Holly Colvin," he said. "Thanks for saving me from Vampira the Sales Queen."

She laughed. "Thanks for making this the most interesting lunch break I've had all week. If Vampira comes back, just tell her I had a family emergency."

"Of course. I'll explain that one of the twins threw up at daycare."

"Twins?"

He nodded. "We're married, right? Might as well toss a couple kids into the mix to make it believable."

A chill raced through her body, and Holly fought to keep the smile pasted in place. "Right. The all-American dream with the kids and the power-hungry career man and the subservient, stay-at-home mommy in an apron. Just text me with whatever you want for dinner, sweetums."

He blinked. "What?"

"Nothing." She grinned to show him she wasn't crazy, even though the jury was still out on that one. "It was great meeting you, buddy. Good luck with the new job."

She turned and walked away, feeling his eyes on her and kinda enjoying the sensation. It wasn't until she got halfway to her car that she realized she hadn't even asked his name.

Just as well, she told herself, shrugging her leather tote higher onto her shoulder. *The last thing you need is another career-driven workaholic looking for a wifey to chain to his stove. Been there, done that, burned the ill-fitting T-shirt.*

She slung herself into the driver's seat of her red Volkswagen Beetle and clicked her iPod until she found something suitably loud and upbeat. She listened to Foster the People on high volume for the twenty-minute drive back to the office, enjoying the sunny fall weather and the spicy smell of leaves blowing through her open car windows.

It was almost enough to make her forget the meeting

she'd been dreading all day. The meeting she'd dreaded for two years, come to think of it.

But the closer she got to her office, Holly felt herself shifting back into career mode. She had two hours until the appointment with her loan officer. There was a lot to get done between now and then.

By the time she walked through the door of First Impressions, the warmth she'd felt from her encounter with Magic Hands had all but faded. She had real business to deal with here, and today sure as hell wasn't the day to get distracted by a sexy geek. If things didn't go well with the bank, it wasn't just her business that might fall apart. For Holly, this business was her whole life.

She ran a hand over the stylized purple reception desk, its retro chrome legs gleaming against the mosaic tile floor that lined the reception area. She'd picked this table out herself, along with all the rest of the furnishings. She and her best friend, Miriam, had worked hard to build First Impressions from the ground up, and not a day went by that Holly didn't feel ridiculously proud about it.

Proud and *lucky*. There was still a risk she could lose it. Hell, she'd nearly lost it all two years ago.

How was she supposed to know her husband would go from sweet and supportive to resentful of her career before the ink had dried on the marriage license?

But she'd kept moving along these last two years, adding clients and employees and figuring out how to pay all the bills along the way. They were on the brink of becoming the largest PR and branding firm in the whole city, with a wall full of awards for their work.

Lucy the receptionist looked up from her computer and smiled. "Did you have a good lunch?"

"Not bad," Holly said. "Drank a protein shake, squeezed some pillows, made out with a strange man in a furniture store."

"All in a day's work," Lucy called as Holly ducked around the corner into her office.

She dropped into her custom-fitted Aeron chair and tapped her keyboard to bring up her calendar. She had a meeting at one thirty with the owner of a destination marketing organization looking for a new branding campaign. After her appointment at the bank, she had a phone conference to coach a hospital administrator on some public speaking tips, and after that—

"Holly?"

Lucy's voice over the phone's intercom system jolted her from her planning. "Yes?"

"There's a call for you on line three. A Ben Langley?"

"Did he say who he's with?"

"He didn't, but he asked to speak with you directly. Would you like me to put him through to your voicemail?"

"That's okay," Holly said, reaching for the receiver. "It's probably one of the guys from that lemonade company. They keep adding new people to tomorrow's meeting agenda."

"Got it. Here you go." Lucy clicked off, and Holly hit the button to take the call.

"Hello, this is Holly Colvin."

"Holly Colvin," he repeated as though tasting the words, and Holly's brain flashed on an image of the guy in the furniture store. His voice was as warm and broad as his hands on her back, and her spine tingled at the sound.

"This is Ben Langley, the new CEO of Langley Enterprises. We met at the furniture store?"

"Ben, of course. Lovely to hear from you." She crossed her legs under the desk and plucked a green ballpoint pen from the ceramic mug on her desk. "What can I do for you?"

"Quite a lot, actually," he said, his voice low and rumbly. "I need you. I *want* you."

Chapter Two

Holly dropped her pen. It bounced once, then rolled off the end of her desk as Ben's words echoed in her head.

I need you. I want you.

Her traitorous heart pulsed in her chest, though it wasn't the only thing throbbing. She uncrossed her legs, then crossed them again, her palms slick at the memory of Ben's mouth on hers.

"Pardon me?" she said, smoother than she felt, but she wasn't a pro at this PR business for nothing.

"I need a PR firm," he said evenly. "And I've done a bit of research on your website in the last twenty minutes, and I've come to the conclusion that I want it to be *you*."

"Me, right, yes—First Impressions," Holly said, scrambling to pick up her pen as she chided herself for reading too much into his words. "Of course. What is it you had in mind, Mr. Langley?"

"Ben. Call me Ben, please." He cleared his throat, and she remembered the feel of rough stubble against her cheek.

"Okay, Ben," she said. Hey, she'd call him whatever he

wanted her to. Rule number one was putting clients at ease, letting them know they could trust her. If being on a first-name basis was what did it for *Ben*, so be it. "What is it you'd like us to do for you?"

"I've been instructed to attend a corporate function at seven thirty this evening, and in the words of my father, 'mingle, schmooze, hobnob, and chinwag.' I had to google two of the four terms. In case you failed to notice, I'm not exactly a people person."

She couldn't figure out if he was joking or not, but he didn't seem like the sort to make wisecracks. "So you need help with your professional networking skills?"

"Among other things. It was suggested to me by my best friend, Parker, that I have the charm of a porcupine with the flu."

Was he really this unaware of his own appeal? The man had charm oozing from his pores, but she couldn't outright argue with him. He didn't seem the type to be helped by that sort of thing. At least not now.

"I see," she said.

"I pointed out that the North American porcupine is actually well-known for its adaptability to unfamiliar habitat, superior swimming capabilities, and relative longevity among most species of rodents. Apparently those aren't selling points for a CEO."

Holly laughed. "You don't say." She tapped her pen on her desk, not certain if the guy had the driest sense of humor on the planet or the most awkward social skills she'd ever encountered. Either way, it was clear he had a few rough edges to smooth. "So let me get this straight," she said. "You want to rebrand *yourself*?"

"In a manner of speaking, yes. We're trying to land a new client whose business could catapult Langley Enterprises into a whole new realm of operations. I have until the end of the month to demonstrate I'm prepared to take us there."

"The end of the month?" Holly swallowed and glanced at her calendar. Nothing like a deadline to really up the stakes. "What's happening at the end of the month?"

"The biggest sales presentation we've ever done, preceded by a whole lot of wining and dining between now and then."

"I see."

"Look, I'm confident I have the brain to be a CEO," Ben said. "I just lack the charisma. The ability to speak my mind and make people listen to what I say. But my father is insistent the time has come for me to take the helm of the family business now that he's shifting to a new role."

"Langley Enterprises is your family business?"

"My great-grandfather started it. My grandpa became president after him, and then my father, and now…"

He trailed off there, his voice sounding a bit glum, and Holly ached to ask for details, but she bit her tongue. It wasn't any of her business.

"The men in my family are charismatic leaders," he said. "My grandfather probably invented the word *hobnob*. I, on the other hand, graduated from Yale at eighteen with honors and with the dubious distinction of never having kissed a girl."

"Ah," Holly said, the memory of his kiss prompting her to lick her lips. "Apparently you've had time to hone your skills since then."

He laughed, a deep, throaty tone that made her wonder what sort of sounds he'd make in bed. "That's kind of you to say. You think I should just tongue-wrestle my colleagues at professional functions?"

Oh God…

If those were the kinds of thoughts running through her head, there was no way in hell she should take any job that put her in close proximity with this man. She'd shared one moment with him at the furniture store. As cute as he was—as hot as that kiss had been—this was business. Her career. Her life. She couldn't afford to get mixed up with a client, even if he did make her flush just from the memory of his lips on hers…

"Look, Mr. Langley—"

"Ben."

"*Ben*." Slipup number one. Yet another sign she needed to back off. "I have to be honest. This is a little outside the realm of my normal corporate branding work. I typically develop high-level campaigns to influence the public's perception of a company or a product."

"In this case, consider me the product. I'm the face of the company, and I need help. I've spent the last ten years working my ass off for Langley, but my closest colleagues were protons and polymers."

"I take it the protons and polymers weren't concerned about your hairstyle?"

"What's wrong with my hairstyle?"

"Nothing, if you're into that whole rumpled 'just got out of bed' look."

Which I kinda am.

Holly bit her lip, hoping she hadn't offended him. Hell, maybe she *should* offend him. Maybe then he'd hang up himself and she'd be off the hook. "I don't know that I'd be right for this job," she said at last. "But if you believe First Impressions is the best PR firm for your needs, I can personally select someone from our staff to work with you."

A silence followed for several seconds, and she wondered if the line had gone dead. Maybe he really had hung up.

"Someone else?" he said at last. "I was hoping it would be you. At least with you, I know we already work well together."

Yeah. That was kind of the problem. If that kiss was any indication, they worked a little *too* well together.

"Besides," he continued before she could voice another

objection. "I reviewed the bios for your whole staff on the website. There's no one else on your team with the same mix of skills you have in corporate branding, public speaking—"

"Ben, I'm sorry, the situation would simply be too... *unusual*."

She let the word hang there between them for a moment, hoping he understood what she was driving at. Then again, even Holly wasn't sure what she was driving at. Why was it so terrifying to imagine mixing business with a guy she found so attractive?

You know damn well why.

He cleared his throat. "If it's a matter of money, I can assure you, I'll pay whatever fee you think is necessary. Triple it if you think the assignment is *unusual* enough to warrant it."

She grimaced and tapped her pen on the desk. The money was tempting, but she wasn't that desperate. Was she? She closed her eyes. "I'm sorry. But I'm sure you'll find a PR firm that's more suited for your needs. Good luck to you."

Then she hung up before that sexy voice could talk her into something entirely more dangerous than a job.

Like his bed.

Chapter Three

Two hours later, Holly sat numb in the office of a loan officer at her bank. In one hand, she gripped a tepid cup of weak tea. In the other, she clutched the paperwork spelling out her worst nightmare.

"But I don't understand," she said. "My divorce papers clearly state that I retain ownership of First Impressions. The business, the building—all of it belongs to me and my business partner."

The loan officer gave her a sympathetic look and shuffled her own pile of paperwork. "That may be what your divorce decree says, but a divorcing couple can't make an agreement that's legally binding on a third party like a bank."

Which her ex-husband, Chase, would have known, since he was a goddamn lawyer.

Holly bit her lip. "My ex signed a Quit Claim relinquishing any rights to the property. He's never paid a dime toward any of it—not the down payment or the monthly payments or any taxes or interest—it's all come straight from my account."

"Yes, but his name is still on the mortgage. That's a

separate thing from being on the title."

"I know that," she said, trying her best to remember all the details they'd hashed out during the divorce. Her throat was growing tight, and it was getting tough to breathe. "But since the economy did a nosedive just a couple months after I started First Impressions, and then we divorced right after that, there was no way to refinance the loan to remove his name. The loan was underwater, even though I always made the payments on time and in full."

"Yes, that's how it happened for a lot of people."

Which didn't help Holly at all. She looked down at the paperwork again and ordered herself to keep breathing. "My ex-husband and I agreed I'd refinance and get his name off the loan as soon as the real estate market bounced back enough that it wasn't underwater anymore."

"A sound idea, but it appears your ex has changed his mind."

Not the first time.

Panic inched its way up her spine.

"I don't understand why he's doing this," she whispered. "We had an agreement."

She should have known better than to believe he'd hold up his end of the deal. Hell, she should have known better than to have Chase co-sign the loan in the first place when she decided to start First Impressions. But they'd been *married*, for crying out loud, and the bank hadn't been willing to loan that much in her name only.

"Maybe someone else could co-sign on a new loan with you," the loan officer suggested. "A parent, maybe, or —"

"No, my parents don't have that kind of money, and my business partner had some previous credit challenges that make it impossible for her to co-sign." She took a sip of her tea, then choked a little as she tried to force it past the lump in her throat. The paper cup felt soggy in her hand, which was also how her brain felt at the moment.

"This makes no sense," she said. "From day one, I was the only one making the payments. Chase realized right after First Impressions opened that it was going to mean *more* hours of work for me, not fewer, and he started badgering me to give it up and—"

She broke off there, her voice choked with unshed tears. This wasn't the loan officer's business. Holly had to be strong. She had to show she was a competent, professional business owner who could handle the curveballs her career threw at her.

But the curveballs from her ex-husband—well, those were something different.

"I'm sorry, Holly, but refinancing or selling might be your only options."

She swallowed back the lump in her throat. "I've tried everything to refinance. You know that. With the real estate market down, the value of the building is less than what I owe, so the bank won't let me refinance even though I've never missed a payment."

And selling isn't an option. At current market prices, I'd lose everything I've sunk into this business, plus First Impressions would be homeless and all my employees would be out of work and—

"I'm sorry," the loan officer said again. "If you could come up with a bigger down payment, they might let you refinance."

"How big are we talking?"

The loan officer flipped through her paperwork and frowned. "Remember the retainer you deposited three weeks ago for that new client?"

"Yes."

"At least triple that."

She dropped the empty paper cup. It bounced off the edge of the desk and landed in her lap, dribbling lukewarm droplets of tea on her leg.

At least triple.

Was that even possible?

In response, she heard the echo of Ben's voice.

"I'll pay whatever fee you think is necessary," he'd told her on the phone. *"Triple it if you think the assignment is unusual enough to warrant it."*

She grabbed the soggy paper cup and gripped it tight in her hand. *Ben.*

Could she really turn down the chance to save her business based on the fear she couldn't control herself around Ben Langley? All the guy needed was a little help tapping into that alpha male CEO she'd glimpsed lurking inside him. He wanted professional rebranding, not an excuse to roll around naked with her.

Her thoughts veered dangerously with that mental picture—all that heat and muscle and sweat—which was probably a bad sign right off the bat.

But she forced herself to focus. All she had to do was stay professional. To do the job Ben hired her to do, then tell him good-bye once they finished their business. No illicit hookups, no messy relationships, nothing to undo all this hard work she'd put into building First Impressions from the rubble of her divorce. She'd learned her lesson already, hadn't she?

She licked her lips and regarded the loan officer. "How long do I have?"

The woman steepled her hands on the desk. "Thirty days."

Holly nodded, then stood on shaky legs and stuffed the paperwork in her bag. "I'll find a way to do this."

She turned and walked out of the office, hoping like hell she wasn't too late to take Ben up on his offer.

•••

"Ben, my boy!"

Ben looked up from his computer to see his father marching into his office wearing a purple polo shirt and plaid pants so hideous they had to be either very trendy or very expensive. Probably both.

Lyle Langley clapped Ben on the shoulder hard enough to knock his glasses askew, which was no small feat considering Ben was a good six inches taller than his dad.

Probably why he always slugs you when you're sitting down, his subconscious pointed out.

He straightened his glasses, squared his shoulders, and turned to face his father. "What's up, Dad?"

"How about we get out there and play nine holes before the Kleinberger dinner?"

"Nine holes?" Ben repeated, trying not to stare at the pants.

His father frowned. "Golf. In golf you can either play nine holes or—"

"I understand how golf works," Ben said, knowing that was only partly true. He'd done it enough times to keep up on the course, and he'd read several books on the game so he could hold his own in golf chatter with his father's colleagues. But honestly, the thought of playing even one hole right now made Ben want to slug himself in the forehead with a nine-iron.

"The boys from Kleinberger wanted to hit the ball around a little while they're in town," his father continued, picking up Ben's paperweight and tossing it from one hand to the other. "Good opportunity for you to get acquainted, let them see Langley Enterprises is going to be in good hands with you at the helm of domestic relations."

"And you think my golf swing is the key to that?"

His dad frowned and stopped tossing the paperweight. "As opposed to your shining personality?"

"Point taken," Ben said, annoyed the barb stung as much as it did.

"You've gotta step up now, son," Lyle said, his voice turning serious. "It's time to stop screwing around with your face buried in a book and prove you're a real Langley."

"Sure thing, Dad," he said, wishing he sounded more like an authoritative leader and less like a nerdy middle school kid who'd dropped his science project in the parking lot. One more thing Holly could have helped him with.

"Look—I really need to go over these spreadsheets before the end of the day," Ben said. "I think I've pinpointed a couple areas where I might be able to save Langley Enterprises several hundred thousand dollars in translation and localization for our foreign sales."

He watched his father's eyes light up, and he felt a rush of relief at having finally found a common language with the old man.

"A few hundred thousand, eh?" He clapped Ben on the shoulder again and grinned. "Atta boy. You keep at it then. You'll be at the event tonight, right?"

"Right. I'll be there."

"Not alone, I hope. Wouldn't be my son if you don't show up with a woman on your arm."

"Right," Ben said, willing himself not to think of Holly again. "I'll see what I can do."

"Go, Benny Boy!" If his dad looked pleased at the thought of money, he looked like he might be on the brink of wetting himself at the idea of Ben having a date. "Make sure she's a looker. Appearances matter in business, you know. Gotta show the Kleinberger guys you're the sort of man who strolls in with a good-looking female."

"In that case, maybe I could borrow my buddy's cocker spaniel," Ben offered. "Daisy could always use a good walk."

"Don't be cute with me. Dating an attractive woman is

a smart career move. You think I got where I did by making dumb business decisions?"

The fact that his father regarded the opposite sex as a business commodity was depressing as hell to Ben, but now didn't seem like the time to argue.

And yeah, he had to admit he'd noticed those lush curves under Holly's blouse and the way her eyes widened as he'd touched his lips to hers. He remembered the urgent way she'd pressed her whole body against him when he'd kissed her.

Yet another reason to regret that she'd rejected his offer.

"Here's another business tip from your old man," his dad said, and for a startling moment, Ben thought his father planned to offer him kissing pointers. But no, Lyle was still talking business. Of course. "To get a woman like that," his dad said, "you've got to wine her and dine her. Take her out someplace nice, buy her jewelry every now and then."

"I'll take that under advisement," Ben said, thinking of his mother. He remembered walking into the living room at fifteen to see her looking sadly down at a diamond tennis bracelet.

"That's nice," Ben had said, hoping to cheer her up.

"Thanks," she'd said, swiping at the corner of her eye. "Your father can't make it for our anniversary dinner, but he sent this."

Ben had nodded, taking a closer look at the bracelet and realizing it was the same damn one he'd sent her the year before. And the year before that. And the year before *that*.

Even then, he'd known his mother would have given all the diamonds in the world for a quiet night on the sofa snuggling with her husband eating popcorn and watching movies.

Truth be told, that was Ben's idea of a perfect evening, too.

"So you're sure I can't get you out on the golf course with

the Kleinberger execs?" his father said.

"I'd love nothing more," Ben lied. "But business calls."

His dad frowned and shook his head, but he must have seen there was no changing Ben's mind. "Okay then. See you in the Jefferson Room at seven thirty."

"I wouldn't miss it for the world."

Another lie so bad it almost hurt his tongue to spit the words out. God, this was going to be harder than he thought. The words coming out of his mouth sounded nothing like his own, but they seemed to be a requirement of the job. How could he convince people he was this powerful CEO if he didn't believe it himself?

He waited until his dad strode from the room before slouching back into his chair. He turned back to his laptop and pulled up a spreadsheet on Langley's international manufacturing operations.

But he didn't find the usual focus that came to him when he immersed himself in data and spreadsheets. Maybe it had been wrong to take this CEO gig. Maybe he was trying to be someone he couldn't be even if he wanted.

His dad's words echoed in his head. *You've gotta step up now.*

Ben knew exactly what he meant by that. He'd seen Lyle demonstrate it at the country club countless times, a glass of scotch in one hand, the other hand greeting strangers with an anaconda death grip as his dad flashed his most charming smile.

God, there weren't enough Crest Whitening Strips in the world for Ben to pull off that smile, much less the handshake. Or any of it, for that matter. What the hell was he doing here?

You're seizing the chance to run this company your way. You've just gotta hone your leadership skills first.

Ben had no intention of following the Langley tradition of being an all-around grade-A asshole when it came to human relationships, especially with women. That seemed to be par for the course among Langley CEOs, and Ben had spent years watching his dad break his mother's heart again and again with short-skirted secretaries and questionable business trips and long work hours that left no time for them to spend any quality time together.

If that was part of the job, Ben would just as soon light his desk on fire and crawl under it right now.

But he could do it his way, he was almost sure of it. He just needed charm and people skills to pull it off. Holly had seemed like the perfect person to help him out with that, but she'd turned him down. He'd gotten off the phone with her hours ago, but he still couldn't shake her final words to him.

Good luck!

"I'll need a helluva lot more than luck if I have to do this on my own," he said aloud, then grimaced. Talking to himself was probably one of those habits he'd need to break in his new position. It was one thing to sit at your home office all day muttering about non-oxide ceramics. It was another to do it with a secretary sitting fifteen feet away and a whole building full of people occupying the nine floors below him at the Langley headquarters.

The phone rang, and it took him a few beats to realize it was his personal line and not his desk phone. He fumbled the iPhone out of his pocket, knocking a clump of nachos into his lap in the process.

"Parker," he said, reading his buddy's name off the screen as he lifted the phone to his ear. "I was just talking about you. Well, your dog."

There was a long pause, and Ben thought he heard his best friend give a snort of dismay. "If Daisy is your idea of a good topic of workday conversation with business executives, I shudder to think what you'll come up with for cocktail party banter. Squeaky toys? Root canals? The mating habits of woodland beetles?"

Ben sighed. Normally, Parker's ribbing wouldn't bother him. Hell, he'd probably dish some right back at him. But this day was turning out to be anything but normal. He looked at his watch, and it dawned on him he'd missed his regular workout date. "Sorry I couldn't make it at lunch," he said. "My gym time is going to be a bit limited for the foreseeable future."

On the other end of the line, his best pal snorted. "It's your first day as CEO and you're already turning into your dad?"

Ben grimaced, wishing the words didn't make him want to stab himself in the eye with his letter opener. "That's kind of the point, isn't it?"

"Then it's my job to balance you out. I just signed us up to volunteer with that charity group that teaches boxing to underprivileged kids. You're welcome. And you're sparring with me and Mike and Justin at noon tomorrow, so don't bail again."

"Fine," Ben said, glancing at his calendar. He should probably protest, but beating the hell out of a punching bag or one of his sparring partners was the only thing that kept him sane sometimes. He kinda liked having a hobby that kept him in shape and kept him from descending into total pocket-protector geekdom.

"So are you wearing ugly golf pants and barking orders at strangers yet, or have you not fully transitioned into becoming your dad?"

"I'm working on it," Ben grumbled.

"You don't sound so sure of yourself."

"Oh I'm sure of myself. One hundred percent." Words said as much to convince himself as Parker. "I'm actually looking into hiring someone to help me out a little."

"You mean like a life coach or something?"

"Or something," Ben agreed, trying not to feel too glum that Holly had turned him down. Hopefully he could find someone else.

I don't want anyone else.

Ben cleared his throat. "Look, I've gotta go. I have to get ready for this big event with the Kleinberger execs. But I'll do my best to make it tomorrow."

"Twelve thirty," Parker said. "Be there."

Ben hung up and shoved his phone back in his pocket. He turned back to his computer, eager to return to the sea of numbers and data that always gave him comfort. He'd just flicked his screensaver off when he heard footsteps.

His secretary's voice came from the intercom. "Ben? There's a Holly Colvin here to see you."

A satisfying jolt of energy coursed from his gut to the rest of his extremities, and he took his hand off the keyboard long enough to punch the intercom button on his phone.

"Really?"

"That's what she said."

Hot damn. "Thanks, Carol. You can send her in."

He turned back to his computer, determined to finish one last calculation. He could hear footsteps behind him, but he had to tally up the figures for the—

"No," the voice said behind him. "Are you kidding me? No. Just—*no*!"

...

Holly stood in the doorway, studying her new client. At least she *hoped* he'd be her new client.

Please say the offer is still good…

Right now, though, she had more pressing concerns. Ben had kicked off his shoes, which revealed one brown sock with red and blue stripes and one black sock with gray checks. The only thing about them that matched was the fact that both had holes in the toes.

His shirt was even more wrinkled than it had been in the furniture store, which was saying something. There was a smear of something orange on his sleeve, which she guessed might be cheese from the half-eaten plate of nachos on the edge of his desk. His hair was rumpled and his glasses were slightly askew, though those details gave him a sexy professor vibe she wished wasn't so damn hot.

This is bad.

He hadn't been wearing a jacket when they'd met earlier, but she could see one hanging on the back of his chair, its corduroy sleeves and beige elbow patches making her cringe at the thought that he'd worn it anytime in the last decade.

Really bad.

"What's the matter?" he asked.

"I honestly have no idea where to start." She looked at her watch. "The event is at seven thirty?"

"Yes."

"You weren't planning to go there straight from work, were you?"

"Of course. Is there a problem?"

"A problem," she repeated, too dumbfounded by his appearance to sugarcoat her words the way she normally would with a new client. "You're planning to show up at your first corporate event wearing holey socks, a cheese-stained shirt, and a jacket that looks like you kidnapped a retired librarian and ripped it off his back?"

"The librarian's tied up in the coat closet," Ben deadpanned, and Holly tried not to notice how stupid-sexy it was. "I promise I'll let him out after the event."

She shook her head. "Ben, you can't attend a corporate function like that."

He cocked an eyebrow and gave her a smile that was half

puppy-dog hopeful, half self-satisfied smirk. God, she wished that weren't so hot.

"Is that why you're here?" he asked. "You changed your mind about taking me on as a client?"

"Yes," she said. "If the offer still stands."

"It stands. It definitely stands. What changed your mind?"

Holly hesitated. *I'm desperate for money* was hardly the right answer. Neither was, *I'm pretty sure I can keep myself from groping you.*

She cleared her throat. "I don't like to turn down clients with such an urgent need."

"I definitely have an urgent need."

You and me both, buddy.

She folded her arms over her chest and tried to look professional. "First things first," she said. "Your clothes."

He looked at her for a few seconds, like he was considering this new option. He seemed to come to a decision, then, because he looked down at his shirt and shrugged. "I think there's a spare shirt stuffed in my gym bag."

"You have an iron in there, too?"

He gave her a funny little half smile that made her feel like she'd just swallowed a ball of sunshine.

"I'm getting the sense you have concerns about my wardrobe."

She sighed. "Ben, it's important to make a good first impression. What sort of impression do you think you're going to make if you walk in there looking like a homeless guy?"

"That I care more about the company's bottom line than what I'm wearing?"

"A nice thought, but no." She shook her head. "A man walks into a room looking like he dressed himself while blindfolded and people are not going to think, 'Wow, I bet he's really good with numbers.' They're thinking, 'Wow, do I trust a guy to put together a million-dollar business deal when he can't even put together a matching pair of socks?'"

"Ouch."

He didn't look terribly pained, but she softened her tone anyway. "Look, you're not paying me to pat you on the head and give you a lollypop. You're paying me to fix what's not working."

"Is it too late to get the lollypop?"

"Ben—"

"I know, I know." He held up his hands in mock surrender. "I get it, I do. I need help. That's what I'm paying you for." He nodded at the folder she'd forgotten she was holding. "Is that the contract?"

"Yes." She held it out to him, and an electric current sizzled up her wrist as his fingers brushed hers. "Speaking of paying me, I took you up on your suggestion to triple the regular fees, due to the *unusualness* of the situation."

She held her breath, waiting for his reaction. He opened the folder and studied the forms, his amber-flecked eyes moving back and forth over the words.

Feeling nervous, Holly swallowed hard. "The retainer is high, but I can assure you it includes a comprehensive action plan beginning with—"

"It's fine," he said, pulling a pen out of a dirty-looking coffee mug and scrawling his signature on the form. Holly stared at his hands, wondering if he'd ever played football or wrestled grizzly bears. He had huge hands. Man hands. Big, beautiful, magical hands designed for gripping and squeezing and stroking and—

"Shall we get started?"

He looked up at her, and she tried to remember what they were talking about. "Wh—what?"

"With the action plan," he said, cocking his head to the side and studying her with an expression that made her wonder if he knew she'd been fantasizing about his hands all over her body. "The terms you've outlined here are acceptable, and I'll have a check to you first thing in the morning for the first half. I'm ready to get a jump on this."

So am I, Holly's body telegraphed as her gaze fell to his hands again.

Fortunately, her brain had the good sense to override it.

"Yes. Absolutely, of course." She cleared her throat and met his eyes. "First things first, Ben. Let's get you out of those clothes."

Chapter Four

Holly glanced at her watch as she leaned against the wall outside the dressing room at the trendy men's clothing boutique. She'd texted Miriam from the elevator at Ben's office seeking emergency advice on men's business attire.

Luckily, her business partner was also First Impressions' resident fashionista. Miriam had come through in spades, texting oodles of shopping tips, the name of her favorite boutique, and a dozen screenshots of men's clothing.

He'll look super-hot in this, read the text accompanying one photo.

That's the understatement of the millennium, Holly thought as Ben stepped out of the dressing room and ambled toward her. He wore a charcoal and turquoise stripe worsted wool Sartorial two-button suit from Armani, something Miriam had expressly told her to look for. The salesman had been happy to comply, and from what Holly had seen of the price tag, she couldn't blame the guy for getting giddy.

But she couldn't blame herself, either, for wanting to climb Ben like a cat tree now that she'd seen him in the suit.

He looked sexy, refined, and utterly, deliciously handsome.

Keep your eye on the prize.

This was a business relationship. Nothing more. That kiss notwithstanding. Not that she hadn't replayed it in her mind a dozen times in the last hour, his mouth hot and demanding on hers as his hands moved up her body…

Before she could make a move—thankfully—the sales assistant scurried over and began fussing over Ben.

"Oh, that's just fabulous," gushed the dapper young clerk wearing a bright orange tie and an engraved silver tag that indicated his name was Marcus. He adjusted the sleeves of Ben's jacket, clucking to himself as he stepped around to survey him from the other side. "The shoulders will need to be let out a little bit, but we have an amazing tailor who can have it done in a jiffy. How do you like that tie?"

"It's, uh—a tie," Ben said, tugging at his collar. "Is it supposed to feel like I'm being strangled?"

Holly laughed and stepped forward, hesitating a moment before reaching out to adjust the knot at his throat. It clearly didn't need any adjusting, but she kept doing it anyway just to feel the warmth of his skin through the blue cotton shirt. "Have you never worn a tie before?"

"Only for funerals and weddings. Oh, and for Halloween one year."

"Halloween? What was your costume?"

"Dirty Harry." He made a pistol with his thumb and forefinger and pointed it at the mirror. "'*Do you feel lucky, punk?*'"

She shivered, flustered by the unexpected show of masculine charm. She compensated by running her fingers down the tie to smooth out imaginary wrinkles. "It looks good on you," she said, trying not to notice the swell of his chest. "It's a nice color."

"The pants are a great fit," Marcus said, giving Holly an

excuse to look down and admire the fit of the inseam. Or admire something, anyway.

Wow, flat-front slacks don't leave a lot to the imagination...

"How does that length feel?"

She tore her gaze off his crotch and blinked at the clerk. "What length?"

"The pants." Marcus gave her a tiny smirk before looking up at Ben. "I think they're perfect, but some men prefer about a quarter-inch longer."

"Longer, right," she babbled, feeling like an idiot. "Um, finding the right length can be hard." Shit. "Not *hard* in the sense that—"

"I think I'll defer to your judgment on the pants," Ben said to the clerk before yanking on the tie again.

She took a step back so she wouldn't do something stupid like grab his ass.

Ben looked away from her and turned to the mirror, pivoting to check out his reflection. "I don't suppose there's any chance of having the jacket altered in time for an event this evening? I'm happy to pay extra, of course."

"Let me go have a chat with the tailor and see what we can do," Marcus said, whipping out a measuring tape. "Can you turn for me just a little? There you go. Wow, you're certainly a big fellow, aren't you?"

Ben said nothing, but Holly felt her face grow hot and ordered herself to keep her gaze above Ben's waist. Was she imagining things, or did everything out of anyone's mouth sound like a phallic reference?

"That's a little stiff, isn't it?"

She coughed, then regained her composure when she saw Marcus adjusting the collar of Ben's dress shirt.

"It is a bit stiff," Ben agreed, meeting her gaze in the mirror. He gave a small smile, and she hoped like hell he had no idea what she was thinking.

God, she just needed to stop looking at him. She turned to study a rack of women's clothing behind her so she wouldn't risk letting her gaze drop to the front of Ben's pants. She flipped blindly through the garments, not really seeing any of the slacks or skirts or blouses as the temperature of her cheeks slowly returned to normal.

"That would look outstanding on you, sweetheart," Marcus said behind her.

Holly stopped flipping and froze with her hand on a blue silk dress with a plunging neckline.

"It's totally your color," Marcus added. "That's our last-chance rack. There's only one left."

She glanced at the tag and realized it was in her size. She hesitated, stroking the edge of the cap sleeve. "It's lovely."

"It's a total steal at that price," Marcus said. "That bias hemline would show off those gorgeous legs of yours, too."

"Get it," Ben said, startling her with the directness of his words. She looked up and saw an expression of mild embarrassment on his face. "If you want to, I mean," he said. "My treat. Since you're stuck accompanying me to the event tonight, it's the least I can do."

"I couldn't possibly—"

"I mean it," he said. "I owe you. You had to rearrange your whole schedule just to fit me in."

"I guess I could try it on." She looked at the dress again. She bit her lip, not sure how she felt about the idea of a man choosing her clothing. She remembered Chase laying out dresses at the end of the bed, intent on telling her exactly what to wear to his next office party.

Then again, this blue silk dress was much more her style than Chase's picks had been.

No harm in just trying it on…

She looked at Marcus. "Can you point me to the women's fitting room?"

"Right over there," he said, pointing down the hall. "We'll just finish up here and I'll run the jacket down to the tailor."

Holly held up the dress. She didn't usually accept expensive gifts from clients, but she could always insist on paying for it herself. She hesitated. "I guess it won't hurt to try it on. You'll be okay here for a minute?"

"As long as you approve of what I'm wearing as a viable option for tonight," Ben said.

"It's perfect," she said, swinging her gaze back to him and feeling glad to have a legitimate, work-related reason for checking him out. "You look very sharp."

"It's not too—I don't know. Fussy?"

"Definitely not. You look like a well put together professional. Very CEO-like."

He frowned at himself in the mirror, then nodded. "I look like my father."

There was an edge to his voice, and Holly watched his eyes darken in his reflection.

"Is looking like your father not a good thing?"

He met her eyes again. "Depends on the situation, I suppose."

"A corporate event?"

He sighed. "It's a necessary evil."

"Okay then." She smiled and watched the darkness drift from his eyes. "I'll try on the dress and you can go try on the rest of the evil suits."

He smiled and turned away, which gave her the chance to check out his ass. She wasn't sure whether to credit the pants or what was inside the pants, but the man certainly looked amazing. A fact her racing pulse seemed determined to recognize.

She clutched the dress to her chest, hustled to the women's dressing room, and ducked into the closest stall. She undressed in a hurry, not wanting to miss Ben trying on whatever he planned to model next. Part of her hoped it was the nutmeg-colored shirt that matched the color of his eyes.

Most of her knew she shouldn't be thinking about his eyes or his hands or any part of his body that didn't make business decisions.

She shimmied the dress over her head, savoring the feel of the silk gliding over her curves. There was something erotic about the slip and slide of the fabric, or maybe it was just the thought of Ben in a similar state of undress just down the hall. She felt her nipples grow hard and resisted the urge to stroke her palms over them as she turned to face the mirror.

It was a perfect fit. And Marcus was right, it did make her legs look fabulous, if she did say so herself. The strappy designer shoes she'd been wearing all day were perfect with the dress, and she said a silent thank you to Miriam for giving them to her last Christmas. She wouldn't even have to run home before the event. She could go just like this.

She peeled off the dress and pulled on her own clothes as quickly as possible, hoping she hadn't missed Ben's next wardrobe change. She emerged from the dressing room and hurried back into the hall, but there was no sign of him.

"Ben?"

"Yeah?"

"Do you have more clothes you want to show me?"

"Not yet. Working on it."

"I'll wait out here."

She sat down on the bench beside the dressing room to await the next outfit. Did men even call them outfits? She'd have to ask Miriam. While Holly was proud of her skills as a PR and branding professional, she was by no means a fashion expert. This whole job was a little outside her comfort zone, to be honest.

That wasn't necessarily a bad thing.

Her career was one of the most important things in the

world to her, and pushing herself professionally was part of the package. She wanted to do well, to build her skills and her client roster and her list of reasons why she'd made the right decision picking her career over marriage to a man who wanted her to stay home ironing his shirts and popping out babies. A man who'd almost talked her into throwing away her whole career to be the sort of wife he expected.

"You can't have it all, Holly," Chase had insisted. *"A career or a husband and family—you have to pick one."*

So she'd chosen the career. The decision wasn't tough, since Chase was being a controlling jerk by then, but still. She hadn't regretted her choice, but there were times she still wished she *could* have it all.

She glanced at her watch, a little nervous to realize it was already six thirty. They still needed to drive back to Langley headquarters and get Ben changed for the event. Then she had to talk him through a few of the basics on social etiquette and making a good first impression and—

"Uh, Holly?"

The sound of Ben's voice from the dressing room stall jarred her from her incessant planning.

"Yes?"

"I'm having a bit of a problem here."

"What sort of problem?" She stood up, ready to help. "What's wrong?"

"There's a thread or something caught in the zipper. I can't get the pants off."

She hesitated, resting a hand on the wall of the dressing room. "Do you want me to help?"

"You know, this really isn't how I envisioned you offering to remove my pants."

She felt the heat creeping into her cheeks again, torn between the embarrassment of the situation and the thrill of knowing he'd basically just admitted he'd thought about her taking off his pants.

It was a joke. Don't get too excited.

"Should I go find Marcus?"

"Who's Marcus?"

"The clerk. That's what his nametag said, anyway."

"I should pay more attention to stuff like that."

"There's your first lesson in public relations—always look for nametags." She lowered her voice a little and glanced toward the door. "And based on the attention Marcus was paying to you, I get the sense he wouldn't mind taking off your pants. What is it with you and sales clerks?"

Ben muttered something unintelligible that was probably some sort of engineering curse. "I'm about five seconds from whipping out my pocket knife and cutting the damn things off my body."

"Don't do that! They're the only pair in your size and they don't even need to be tailored."

"I've been at this for ten minutes already."

"Are you sure you're sliding it the right way?"

"I have a doctorate in engineering," he muttered. "I'm pretty sure I understand how a zipper works."

She hesitated at the edge of the dressing room, biting her lip. "Do you want me to try?"

She heard the bolt click from the lock, and the door swung open. Holly stifled the urge to gasp. Ben stood there shirtless and barefoot with his hair tousled and wild. His hand was on his fly, his shirt was on the bench, and Holly was in serious danger of drooling on the floor.

He stuck his head out of the dressing room, glancing left and then right. No sign of the clerk. "This is nuts," he said. "How hard can it be to take off a pair of pants?"

"Maybe it's the angle," she said, stepping toward him and trying her damnedest to maintain some professional composure. "Let me take a look."

He took a step back, moving deeper into the dressing room. "Let's do this in here. I'd rather not undress in the middle of the hallway."

"Good point." She followed him inside, making a concerted effort not to stare at his crotch. Then again, wasn't that what she was supposed to be doing?

She let her gaze drop, wondering why it was so hot in this dressing room. Ben's hand was still on his fly, but she could see he'd managed to get the zipper at least partway down.

"Um, could you maybe move your hand?"

"Sorry, yeah."

He slid his hand away, revealing a happy trail that led into the top of a pair of red boxer briefs that appeared to be in much better condition than his socks. Thank God for small miracles.

There's nothing small about what's in those boxer briefs…

She ordered herself to stop entertaining lewd thoughts as she sat down on the bench in front of him, putting herself at eye-level with his crotch. Holy mother of hell, the man had ridiculous abs. She could grate cheese on them. Holly hadn't pegged him as a gym rat, but clearly the man worked out.

Why was it so hot in this dressing room?

She took a deep breath and reached for his fly, ordering herself not to say anything dumb like "great fabric" or "nice body" or "fuck me."

The zipper was stuck at half-mast, so she grabbed hold of it and gave a firm tug downward. Nothing. She pulled up, thinking maybe she could start over from the top. The damn thing didn't budge. She peered closer, trying to figure out what the problem was.

"It looks like there's a thread caught right here," she said, pinching it between her fingernails and giving a tug.

"Can you pull it?"

"I'm trying. I can't get a grip with my nails. You said you

have a pocketknife?"

"I was kidding."

"I have manicure scissors in my other purse, but I left that at home."

Ben squirmed, muscles rippling as he moved. "I think I'm okay without having scissors anywhere near my junk."

"These teeth are really tight."

"I'm also okay without having teeth near my junk." He squirmed again and Holly grabbed his ass without thinking. "Hold still," she said, gripping his butt cheek to make sure it happened. It occurred to her belatedly that this wasn't the best way to establish a professional relationship with a new client, but there wasn't much to do for that now.

"If I just had a pair of tweezers—"

"Is there anything on your key ring?"

"A bottle opener," she said. "Pretty sure there's not much I can do with that." She tugged at the zipper again, conscious of the fact that she still hadn't taken her hand off his ass. "God, it's really stuck."

"I'm going to have to wear these pants every day for the rest of my life with the zipper halfway down."

"Maybe if I just wiggle it—"

"I'm not sure wiggling it is a good idea," he said, his voice sounding strained. She looked up to see his face flushed to a hue somewhere between strawberry and tomato.

"Why not?"

"Because the more you touch me like that, the tighter these pants are getting."

"What? Oh." She bit her lip, suddenly very aware of the considerable bulge straining against the zipper. She'd been trying not to notice, but now that he mentioned it—

"Okay, actually, this might help," she said, struggling to keep her voice steady as she grabbed the zipper again.

"My boner is helpful?"

She snorted, surprised to realize the word *boner* existed in his genius-level vocabulary. "Kind of," she said. "It's stretching the fabric out. If I could just get a grip on the thread." She looked up at him, pretty sure the words she was about to utter were the most inappropriate ones she could possibly say to a client on the first day of a business relationship.

"Would you mind if I used my teeth?"

Ben looked down at her, his eyes flashing with amusement, his five o'clock shadow darker in the dim light of the dressing room. "By all means," he said, dropping his voice to a low growl. "Put your mouth wherever you like."

...

Ben couldn't believe the words that had just escaped his lips. He sounded like some kind of caveman, not like himself.

Then again, wasn't that the point of hiring Holly? To bring out his inner alpha male? He was having trouble remembering right now with her mouth moving warm and soft over his cock.

Okay, so there was a layer or two of fabric between those perfect, lush lips and the hard-on he was pretty sure would burst right through the fly of these damn pants if she kept touching him like this. Maybe that was the solution. Maybe if she just stepped back and took her hands off him, his dick would bust its way out of this mess all on its own.

"Hold on," she murmured, her voice sending a vibration through the zipper. "I think I've almost got it—"

"Take your time," he said, then mentally kicked himself for being a jackass. It sounded like the sort of sexist thing his dad might say. Of course, it was true he didn't want her to rush. No sense breaking the zipper or tearing the fabric or having Holly take her hands off him for any reason whatsoever.

"Oh!" she gasped. "Right there! Almost got it."

Ben closed his eyes and hoped like hell he didn't embarrass himself. God, her mouth was warm. He could feel her breath through the thin cotton of his boxers and his inner pig hoped like hell this procedure would take at least another hour.

"Dammit," she muttered against his fly. "I just had it."

"Is there anything I can do to help?"

"Just hold still."

"My pleasure," he murmured, thinking this whole experience was a lot more pleasure than he'd ever imagined. Hell, if he'd known pants shopping was this much fun, he would have done it years ago.

Of course, it was probably obvious to Holly, too, just how much he was enjoying the experience. He willed his hard-on to go down, but with Holly moving her mouth over his fly, there was little chance of that happening anytime soon.

He glanced down to see the crown of her head level with his hips. Her dark hair shone bright in the dressing room light and Ben had a serious urge to run his fingers through it.

Great idea, dumbass. Stroke her hair while she mouths your cock.

She tipped her head to the side for a better angle, and Ben admired the flutter of her lashes, the softness of her cheek, the flex of her jaw muscles as she worked the thread. Her fingers squeezed his ass, and Ben squeezed his eyes shut, thinking he was seriously going to lose it if she didn't get that thread pretty soon.

"Holly, maybe we should stop—"

"Got it!" She sat back with a look of triumph, her hair tousled and her lipstick smeared. She reached for his fly and before Ben could brace himself again, she gripped the zipper and gave a firm tug. "Voila!" she announced, sliding the zipper up and then down in illustration.

"You got it," he said, hoping he sounded suitably impressed instead of a little disappointed. He shoved his glasses up his nose and offered her a hand up. "Thank you."

"Not a problem." She let him lift her to her feet as she grinned up at him, her eyes glinting with mischief. "All in a day's work."

"I can't say I envisioned that as part of our arrangement when I signed your retainer."

She smiled and squeezed his fingers. "At least now you know I'm willing to go above and beyond to get the job done."

As far as Ben was concerned, she could go above, below, down, up, and perform any sort of job on him at any time. But he nodded and let go of her hand, pausing to straighten his shirt and take a step back from her.

"Okay then," he said. "In the first few hours of acquaintance, I've kissed you, gotten naked a few feet away from you, and had your mouth on my junk. I'd say it's time to take things to the next level."

Holly's eyes went a little wider and she licked her lips. "What's that?"

"Time to meet my dad."

Chapter Five

Ben stepped through the doors of the conference room, making a conscious effort to straighten his posture the way Holly had coached him in his office a few minutes ago. He surveyed the scene, pushing back the wave of dread that hit him as he took in all those jovial faces, the too-loud voices, the conversations he'd really prefer not to join.

"Here, let me straighten your tie," Holly said, stepping around him to make the adjustment he didn't know he needed. Still, the feel of her hands fiddling with the fabric on his chest filled him with an unexpected calm, and he felt a little less dread about the prospect of joining the crowd.

"Any last-minute tips?" he murmured as she smoothed down the tie, then took a moment to adjust the lapels of his jacket.

"Just do like I told you to," she said, her voice soothing and low. "Smile. Introduce yourself to people you don't know. Shake hands firmly. Ask questions about people to show you're interested in making a connection."

"I'm interested in grabbing a drink," he said, eyeing the

bar in the corner. "Can I get you something?"

"A glass of red wine would be great," she said. "Just remember what I said about keeping consumption to a minimum. Think of it as a prop—something to do with your hands, rather than something to guzzle."

Ben had plenty of ideas what he'd like to do with his hands, but he just nodded and practiced holding eye contact with her the way she'd coached him to demonstrate he was paying attention. "Got it. Red wine, walk slowly, don't guzzle."

"And tip well," she said as he started to turn away. "That's another aspect of being charming."

"In that case, I'm already plenty charming." He nodded toward the bar. "Do you want to join me and choose your wine?"

"No, I'd like to observe you in your natural habitat so I can do a better job offering you tips."

"Here's your first tip: This is about as far as it gets from my natural habitat."

She smiled, and Ben felt warmth in his chest. "What's your natural habitat?"

"At home on my couch in a pair of fleece pants with a good beer and a bad sci-fi flick."

"A bad sci-fi flick?"

"One of those old ones that's so bad it's wonderful."

"I can't say I've ever seen any of those."

"I mourn the depths of your deprivation."

"I'll make you a deal then," she said, leaning closer. "Get through this event using all the skills we just talked about and I'll join you for a movie night featuring extra-buttery popcorn and an extra-awful movie."

"Deal," he said, buoyed by the thought of snuggling up on the couch with Holly in skimpy pajamas and her lips glistening with butter. "I'll be right back."

He turned and started across the room, conscious of her

eyes on him. He made an effort to lock gazes with the first person he encountered, offering up the handshake Holly had coached him on—sort of a two-handed maneuver with a hand pump combined with a shoulder clap. It felt more natural than he expected it to, though not nearly as good as it had felt when he'd practiced with Holly in his office.

"Glen, good to see you again," he said, shaking the man's hand and offering up a smile that felt a little too forced. "How's the wife doing?"

The man frowned. "My name's Pete. And I'm not married."

"Right," Ben said, regrouping. "Kids? Pets?"

"I have a ficus tree."

"Excellent. Uh, I hope it's thriving?"

"Sure," the man said, glancing around as though looking for an escape from the conversation. Ben couldn't blame him. "Uh, actually, it's been dropping leaves a bit lately."

"Oh? Yes, I do believe that's common with Ficus Benamina or weeping figs. It can happen if temperatures dip below sixty degrees Fahrenheit or sixteen Celsius." Ben heard the words coming out of his own mouth and knew they weren't what Holly had in mind when she coached him on witty cocktail party banter, but somehow he seemed unable to stop himself. "It can also be a symptom of spider mites. Treatment with a bit of oil from the Azadirachta indica should clear things right up."

Pete blinked at him, then nodded. "Wow, thanks. I'll have to try that—uh, Azardir—"

"Neem oil," Ben said, wondering if Holly was still watching him. If so, maybe he'd get lucky and she'd think he was discussing the fine points of business infrastructure instead of the care and feeding of a houseplant. God, he was such a dork.

But Pete didn't seem to mind too much, and he even

shook his hand again. "Thanks, man. Wow, you're a little different than the last CEO."

"Try not to tell anyone," Ben said, and he turned back toward the bar. Pete didn't know it, but he'd just paid Ben the best compliment he could imagine.

Ben made it a few more feet toward the drink table when a heavyset man in a gray suit stepped in front of him, his face flushed with exertion or maybe too much vodka.

"Ben! Ben my boy, come over here and meet some of the partners."

The man latched onto his arm, and Ben tried to remember if he'd ever met the guy before. He honestly had no idea whether he was about to meet business partners, tennis partners, or sex partners. This was the problem with everyone dressing in dark suits and ties. Everyone looked the same, and Ben had no frame of reference.

The guy dragged him toward a big group of men who all wore some variation of the dark suit and tie, and Ben wished like hell Langley Enterprises had invested in a slew of nametags at functions like this.

The first man hoisted his drink in the air and saluted Ben before turning back to the group. "Everyone, this is the new CEO of Langley Enterprises, Ben Langley. Lyle's his old man, but Lyle's stepping down to take over Langley's international arm. Ben, I'd like you to meet Carl, Jim, Harold, Gary, James, Floyd, Devon, and Jim."

"Uh, two Jims and one James?"

"That's right."

Ben nodded, shaking hands with each man in turn and wondering what these people did and why there were no female executives in the ranks. He was trying to place the first man, knowing they'd probably met countless times before and wishing he was better at placing faces.

"Shame you couldn't join us out on the course today," the

man said, and Ben nodded, grateful to at least have golf as a reference point.

"Right, well, I'm sure my dad showed you a great time out there. You played the Hunter Farms course?"

"Absolutely. Such a terrific Scottish links design out there. Say, listen—have you had a chance to look over the counter-proposal I sent over a couple days ago?"

"Yes, I took a quick look," Ben said slowly, trying to remember if Holly had given him any tips on keeping oneself from telling a business associate that his head was so far up his ass that he might as well inspect his tonsils while he was up there. Ben might not be a social genius, but he suspected that wouldn't be the right way to handle the conversation. "I'll need to do a more thorough review later. Why don't we catch up early next week?"

"Sounds good, my boy!" He clapped Ben on the back and buried his face in his drink again. "Good talking with you."

"You, too."

Ben turned and hurried away, then remembered Holly's advice about carrying himself with confidence and poise. Fuck, he needed that drink. He reached the bar and pulled out his wallet, grateful Holly had urged him to buy a new one when they were standing at the counter back at the clothing store. This one certainly looked better than his old duct-taped one, and the leather smelled woodsy and warm.

"What can I get you, sir?"

"What do you have for red wine?"

"We've got a great Cab from the Napa Valley, this stunning red blend from Rioja in Spain, and a nice little Oregon Pinot Noir—"

"The Pinot would be great," Ben said, glancing back at Holly and wondering if he'd read her right. "Is it a little earthy and spicy?"

"Yes, sir."

"Perfect."

She had her head turned, so he could admire her without self-consciousness from the other side of the room. The blue dress fit her like a dream, hugging her curves and showcasing those perfect long legs. He wasn't usually the kind of guy to openly ogle a woman, but holy hell, how could he not appreciate all that flesh and muscle and—

"Will that be all, sir?"

Ben turned back to the bartender. "Uh, no. What do you have on draft?"

The guy rattled off the names of a few craft beers, and Ben picked the hoppiest IPA on the list.

He pulled a few bills out of his wallet, making sure to include a generous tip and a smile for the bartender. When he had the drinks in hand, he made his way back toward Holly, more excited than he had any right to be at the prospect of standing beside her, having everyone see this beautiful woman next to him.

"Here you go," he said, his fingers brushing hers as he handed her the glass. "I hope you like Pinot Noir."

"I love it," she said, taking a sip. "Wow, this is amazing. Different than what I usually drink. What is it?"

"You're probably used to California Pinots," he said, hoping he didn't sound like too much of a wine snob. When he wasn't sipping beer, wine was his beverage of choice, though he tended to prefer big-bodied reds over the more nuanced French wines his dad collected and seldom consumed.

"Pinot Noir from California or France tends to be a little more polished and refined," Ben explained. "Oregon Pinot, on the other hand—at least the ones I like—are earthy and approachable. A little dirty, if you want to call it that."

"Huh," Holly said, taking a slow sip. "Yeah, I see what you mean. I'm not sure I would have thought of that adjective, but if this is what that tastes like, then I guess I like it dirty."

Ben took a big swallow of his beer and tried not to choke. He surveyed the crowd, catching titters of conversation around him.

"What is it about people in corporate America that makes them talk like androids?" he asked.

"How do you mean?"

"You know—'Let's crosswalk this into our wheelhouse and extrapolate the strategic synergy.' What the hell does that even mean?"

"Not a damn thing, but executives do love their jargon. If it helps, you can turn it into your own secret drinking game."

"A drinking game?"

"Take a sip every time someone says something like 'results-oriented' or 'due-diligence' or 'let's touch base and put our heads together about the action items.'"

Ben laughed and took a small sip of beer. "I'd be wasted in ten minutes, and then I'd be breaking your first rule about minimizing consumption."

"Good point."

Ben glanced around the room and wondered how long he'd have to stay here hobnobbing before he could head upstairs and get out of this goddamn suit. He studied the well-groomed masses drinking a little too much, clapping each other a little too hard on the back.

"Benny boy!" The shoulder clap came from behind, and nearly knocked Ben's drink from his hand. If he hadn't turned at the last second, he might've splashed Holly with beer. The thought of licking it from her cleavage was enough to buoy his spirits for a second, but then he remembered who'd just delivered the blow.

With a heaviness he wished he didn't feel, he turned to greet the shoulder-clapper. "Hi, Dad."

...

Holly watched Ben's smile go from warm and genuine to cardboard-stiff as he turned to greet his father. Another person might not have noticed the shift, but Holly had been admiring Ben's smile all evening, making note of when he looked like he meant it and when he was phoning it in.

Was it wrong to silently celebrate the fact that she seemed to earn the real smile most of the time?

But the smile on Ben's face now looked like he'd just chewed a mouthful of glass and taken a swig of grapefruit juice. Even with the pinched look on his handsome features, the physical resemblance was strong between Ben and his dad. Same broad shoulders, same chiseled jaw, same brown eyes with amber flecks, though there was something about the way Ben's dad's gaze swept her body that made Holly uncomfortable. She and Ben were standing a couple of feet apart, so it was possible the elder Langley didn't even realize they knew one another.

She saw Ben shift his weight, angling his body a little closer to her. From the quick glance he gave to her, then his father, it looked like he was shielding her from his dad's gaze. The rush of gratitude she felt was enough to leave her arms feeling tingly.

"Shoulda been out there on the course with us today, Benny Boy," the older man said, slinging an arm around Ben in a gesture that seemed more like aggression than affection. Holly remembered a documentary she'd watched once about male lions in the wild, and thought about that as she watched the way Ben's father manhandled him while giving a play-by-play of a golf game Ben clearly had no interest in whatsoever.

"But obviously, you were too busy pushing pencils across a desk to get out there and swing the wood around," the elder Langley said, elbowing his son.

Ben opened his mouth to respond to the barb, but Holly beat him to the punch. She slid a hand around his waist, shoved her hand in his back pocket, and gave his ass a small squeeze. It was clear Lyle Langley was a grade-A jerk, and even clearer Ben would prefer not to contradict his dad in public. The least she could do was help Ben play in the same ballpark.

She didn't take her hand off Ben's ass as she turned her best high-wattage smile on his father. "You must be Lyle Langley," she said as she extended the hand that wasn't grabbing Ben's ass. "I've heard so much about you, and it's such a pleasure to finally meet you in person. I'm Holly Colvin."

"Holly," he said, pumping her hand harder than necessary as he stole a glance down the front of her dress. "Well, well, well. I was hoping Ben might bring a lady to the event tonight, but I had no idea he'd managed to round up one so—so—"

"Intelligent?" Ben supplied. "Professional? Charming? Lovely?"

"Yeah, what he said," Lyle answered, seeming to catch himself a bit with his son's gentle reminder that there was more to a woman than tits and ass. The elder Langley cleared his throat. "Nice of you to join my boy here this evening. A powerful man needs a beautiful woman at his side."

"Thank you," Holly said, figuring it was easier to accept the compliment than to dwell on the suggestion that she was nothing more than arm candy. It's not like she'd never been around men who thought that way. Hell, she'd married one.

"So, Mr. Langley," Holly began, but Ben's dad cut her off.

"Lyle," he said. "Call me Lyle, sweetheart."

"Lyle," she replied, glancing up to see Ben's cardboard smile firmly still rooted in place. "Ben was telling me about your remarkable leadership of the company. Tell me, what's the secret to your success?"

The old man beamed like she'd just praised his dick or his car, and Holly knew she'd asked the right question. These business types were all alike, and she hoped Ben was taking mental notes on the inroads to a fellow executive's ego.

"Well, honey," Lyle said, leaning a little closer. "Just between you and me, the secret to success is ball-sack."

Holly blinked. "I beg your pardon?"

"It's an acronym," Ben supplied, not sounding nearly as enthusiastic about it as his father did. "BALSAC. Stands for brains, attitude, luck, skill, aggression, and confidence."

"Served me well my whole life," Lyle said, raising a toast to himself and his BALSAC. "That, and aligning myself with the right sort of people." He gave her another appraising look, this one slightly less lecherous. "Having a sweet, pretty girl by his side can help a man get ahead, too."

Ben edged closer to Holly, which felt like another effort to shield her from his father. "We should probably get going—"

"It's okay," Holly said, giving Ben's ass a reassuring squeeze to let him know she could handle his dad. "You must be very proud of your son following in your footsteps the way he is."

"Absolutely," Lyle said, taking a big gulp from a glass of amber liquid that made Holly's eyes water from three feet away. It smelled like a forest fire, and she wondered what the hell it was. "In a family-run company like Langley, it's all about heritage. Good old-fashioned values and traditions that have made this company great for generations. The good old days were good for a reason, and we like to keep 'em going at Langley Enterprises."

"Sure," Holly said, certain she'd heard a version of this speech coming from her ex-husband's lips not long after they'd returned from their honeymoon.

"There's a reason traditional values are traditional, Holly," Chase had pointed out a few weeks after she and Miriam had opened the doors at First Impressions and he'd realized that having Holly own her own company made her less available to further *his* career by mingling with the other country club

wives. That was right about the time he'd started dropping not-so-subtle hints that she sell her share of the company.

Holly took a slow sip of wine now, conscious of Ben simmering beside her. "Actually, Dad, the good old days weren't always so hot," he said. "Human life expectancy a hundred years ago was only forty-eight, and between poor sanitation and nutrition, it really wasn't—"

"Okay, fine, brainiac," Lyle interrupted. He was smiling at his son, but smile had a hard edge to it. "You know what I meant."

"So look, Dad—I think Holly and I had better get busy mingling, don't you?"

This time, Holly didn't resist Ben's attempt at a rescue. Luckily, Lyle didn't argue, either.

"Sure thing, my boy," he said. "Holly, it's been a pleasure meeting you."

"Likewise, sir."

"Have a good evening, Dad. You can leave some of the hobnobbing to me."

Lyle chuckled and gave Ben an elbow to the ribs. "Get out there and hob some knobs, boy!" he said, tossing back the rest of his drink before ambling off.

Ben shook his head and turned back to Holly. "I'm pretty sure I owe you an apology for at least a dozen aspects of that conversation, but I'm not sure where to start."

She extracted her hand from Ben's back pocket, a little disappointed to break contact with him. "It's okay. I wanted to talk to him."

"Seriously?"

"Well, not for the pleasure of his conversation. More so I could see what you're dealing with. What you're hoping to become."

Ben nodded, looking a little grim. "Right. There's a depressing thought."

"He wasn't that bad," she said, even though she knew damn well he was. "What on earth was he drinking?"

"Laphroaig. You could smell it?"

"The people in the next building could smell it. What on earth is it?"

"It's a single-malt whiskey imported from Islay. Very smoky. My grandfather drank it, and his father before him, and—"

"How do you feel about it?"

"Not good." Ben shrugged and held up his glass. "I'm partial to craft beer."

"Cheers to different tastes, then." She took another sip of wine, feeling her shoulders relax now that Lyle had relocated himself across the room. "So does your mother work in the family business, too?"

Ben's face clouded ever so slightly. "My mother passed away when I was sixteen."

"Oh, Ben—I'm so sorry." She touched his arm, embarrassed to have brought up such a tender subject when he was working hard to play it cool at the event.

But he just nodded, his gaze drifting across the room toward his father. "Thank you. She was an amazing woman. She's one of the reasons I spent a year of grad school researching new developments in chemotherapy."

"She died of cancer?"

He nodded. "Breast cancer. She found a lump, but my dad convinced her it was nothing."

"That's horrible!"

"It wasn't like that, exactly. I mean, he wasn't trying to be a jerk. I think he was in denial. He didn't want anything to shake up this perfect little world he'd built, and my mom didn't want to believe anything could be wrong, either. By the time she finally went to the doctor—" He stopped there and tore his gaze off his father. "Anyway, the chemo was terrible for her. I went with her to all her appointments, and I always thought there had to be a better way."

"That must have been awful for you and your father."

"My father," he repeated, his voice brittle and clipped. She waited for him to say more, but the bitter look he was aiming at his dad told her more than any words could convey. He seemed to catch himself, and he turned back to her. "Anyway, I graduated early from high school right after that and started college at sixteen. I thought I might like to be a doctor, but engineering is where I ended up."

"It seems like it suited you."

"It did. *Does*." He shrugged. "Mom always wished Dad would do more to expand the philanthropic arm of Langley Enterprises. As CEO, maybe I can make that happen."

A light went on in the back of Holly's mind. So *that's* what was driving him to mold himself into CEO material. The chance to do good things with a company that clearly had money to burn. It made sense. "I'm sure your mother would be very proud of you."

"I hope so. How about your parents? Are they supportive of your career?"

"Very. My mom especially. She always stressed how important it was to get an education and be able to support myself without relying on a man."

"Seems like you've been able to do that," he said. "From what I read online about First Impressions, you've been very successful."

"My career has really taken off in the last few years," she agreed, not wanting to dwell on her financial woes with the bank, or on the other aspects of her life where she still wished for more. A relationship, maybe a family—

She cleared her throat. "I feel confident we'll be able to push your career into the next realm with just a few tweaks. Being here tonight is already giving me plenty of ideas for your personal rebrand. I'll get to work on writing up a plan first thing in the morning."

"I can't wait to hear about it."

She nodded, glad to be back on safer ground discussing business instead of personal details. Keeping things efficient and detached was going to be key to staying professional with Ben.

"Okay, so I Facebook-stalked some of the Kleinberger execs when I ran to the bathroom earlier," she said.

He raised an eyebrow at her. "Are you ever *not* working?"

"Not really. Anyway, you should go strike up a conversation with the CEO about his daughter's recent admission to Princeton. He lives for his kids, so he'll appreciate you showing an interest."

"I can't decide if that's creepy or brilliant," he answered, glancing across the room to where Harold was chatting with several other Kleinberger execs.

"How about we go with brilliant?" she suggested.

"Good idea. What did you find out about any of the other execs?"

"Well, Gerald Weisner's wife has been posting a lot of Facebook quotes from narcotics anonymous, so I'm going to go out on a limb here and suggest you not ask about her fondness for Percocet. Also, it's possible their VP just got a hair transplant."

"You found that online?"

"No, just from comparing his 2014 Facebook photos to what he looks like standing over there with that noticeable scar on the back of his head. Also not something you want to mention, by the way."

"Should I be offended that you think I might use drug addiction and plastic surgery as entrees to conversation? I'm socially awkward, but not *that* socially awkward."

"Earlier you called their COO *ma'am*. His name is Bill."

"An honest mistake. You've gotta admit, the pink shirt is a little effeminate."

"Go," she insisted, nudging him toward the Kleinberger execs.

He grinned, clearly not ready to move just yet. "You don't want to come with me and play the doting arm candy role again?"

She felt a dark bubble well up in her chest, and she forced herself not to react. Playing the role of subservient arm candy wasn't the same as being asked to fill that role full time.

She shook her head. "I'll watch from here. It's important to make sure you can handle these kinds of social situations without a woman hanging on your arm."

"I suppose you're right."

They both watched as Lyle Langley walked up to one of the Kleinberger execs and did some sort of obnoxious shoulder-punch routine with a guy in a dark suit.

"So does your dad expect you to handle the company exactly like he does?" she asked.

"I imagine so," Ben muttered. He took a sip of his drink, then turned away and began a slow trudge toward the shark tank. "If I'm not back in ten minutes, send out a search party."

"Will do."

He strode away, and she watched him go, admiring the broadness of his shoulders and the confidence in his handshake as he greeted the execs one by one. After a few minutes of conversation, he glanced back at her and smiled.

The *real* smile.

She felt a warm little shimmy in her belly, and it occurred to her that he might not be completely clueless when it came to professional charm.

• • •

"Are you sure about this?" Holly asked, glancing at her watch as the elevator crawled slowly toward the top floor. "Don't you have to get up early and run the universe or something?"

Ben laughed and leaned against the metal handrail, his posture relaxed and comfortable now that they'd escaped the event. He tugged off his tie and undid the top button of his shirt, giving Holly a welcome glimpse of skin.

"It's only nine fifteen," he said. "I don't have to run the universe for at least a few more hours. Besides, remember what you promised?"

"Right," she agreed, glancing out at the city lights whizzing by outside the glass wall of the elevator. It seemed safer than staring at Ben to see if he'd undo another button. "I know what I promised, but I wasn't thinking you'd take me up on it tonight. It's Tuesday."

He quirked an eyebrow at her. "Is there a reason we can't watch a bad sci-fi movie on a Tuesday?"

"No, I guess not. I just figured we both have to work tomorrow."

He grinned and stuffed his tie in his pants pocket, then tugged at his shirt collar. Grimacing, he undid another button, and she did her damnedest not to stare. "I promise not to keep you out too late," he said. "I'm showing you one of my favorite flicks, not ravaging you on my living room floor."

Holly felt the heat creep into her cheeks and ordered herself to keep a straight face. Okay, fine, the ravaging thing had crossed her mind. Was it that obvious?

She cleared her throat. "I suppose if we start the movie soon—"

"Will you turn into a pumpkin if you're not home before midnight?"

"No, but I might turn into the wicked witch if I don't get out of these shoes soon." She gave an exaggerated grimace, then bent down and rubbed the back of her heel. She hadn't planned on staying out this late when she'd gotten dressed in the morning. She hadn't planned on any of this, really.

She straightened up, shoving her foot back into the shoe. "I thought movie night was going to involve pajamas and popcorn."

"Relax. I've got both of those things waiting for you in my penthouse."

She blinked, not sure she'd heard him right. "You have pajamas?"

"Yep."

"For me?"

"Uh-huh."

"You've got to be at least six-two, Ben. I don't think I'm going to fit in a pair of your old sweatpants."

"I'm six-three, and that's not the plan. You'll have your own pajamas, I promise."

"I can't decide if this is really cool or really creepy."

"Let's go with creepy cool." He nodded down at her feet. "You can take those off if you want. We're almost there, and shoes aren't required in my apartment."

"And you have pajamas waiting for me."

"Yep."

She toed off her shoes and bent down to pick them up. The elevator came to a stop and she straightened as the doors swished open.

"Ladies first," Ben said, gesturing to the opening.

Holly stepped through, feeling Ben close behind her and enjoying it a lot more than she ought to. The floors were white marble and felt cool under her bare feet. The walls were a lush gold brocade that she kinda wanted to reach out and touch. There was an elaborate fountain in one corner, and a front door that looked like it cost more than her whole house.

It was all very beautiful, but none of it looked like Ben.

"Gaudy, isn't it?"

Holly looked back at him. "What?"

"The penthouse. My friend, Parker, calls it the millionaire mausoleum."

"Parker has a point."

"It's one of the perks of this CEO gig, so I guess I can't complain." He stepped past her to shove a key card into the slot beside a massive mahogany door. "If nothing else, it's convenient having a place in the same building as my office."

"I imagine so, if you're a workaholic."

"Guilty as charged."

"Me, too," she admitted. "But I love my job, so I'm not complaining."

"Same here." Ben frowned. "At least I did. I haven't done the CEO thing long enough to fall in love."

"You will," she said encouragingly, hoping it was true.

He shrugged, then shoved the door open. He flicked a light switch, bathing the entry in a pool of warm light. He turned to Holly and smiled. "There's another CEO perk besides the apartment."

"What's that?"

"An administrative assistant who hates social functions almost as much as I do, and who was more than happy to slip out on a quest to purchase a tasteful variety of women's loungewear in your size."

Holly stared at him, not sure whether to be more impressed by his foresight or by the massive slate foyer he'd revealed by pushing open his front door. "Wow." She stepped through the entry, resisting the urge to touch a marble statue or the textured wallpaper or Ben's abs. She settled for keeping her hands to herself. "Impressive."

The compliment applied to the game plan, the apartment, and the abs, though she was pretty sure Ben didn't take it that way.

"Thanks," he said. "None of it's really mine. It comes with

the job, but it's not really me, you know?"

Oddly enough, Holly was pretty sure she did know. This place didn't look like Ben, but she checked it out anyway as she padded barefoot to the edge of a cream-colored plush carpet that seemed to extend for miles. She peered into the room, noticing there wasn't a speck of furniture anywhere. Just a massive television the size of a small car.

"Here's the downside," he said, stepping up behind her. "None of the furniture I ordered has been delivered yet, so we're going to have to make do without it. Are you okay sitting on the floor?"

"Do you have bedding?"

He cocked an eyebrow at her. "Are you proposing a slumber party?"

She laughed and tried to ignore the flush spreading through her body at the thought of getting into bed with him. Crap, maybe this wasn't such a great idea.

"I just meant we could make a cozy nest of blankets and pillows on the floor," she said. "Seems like the perfect way to watch a movie."

"Deal," he said. "You get your PJs. I'll get the popcorn going. We can make the blanket fort together."

"You really do think of everything, huh?"

"I try," he said with a grin. "Carol said she'd leave the shopping bags in the powder room over there. Pick whatever you like and join me in the living room when you're ready."

Holly moved past him, not sure how she felt about a guy planning everything about what she'd wear or how she'd spend her evening. Part of her wanted to be annoyed. Wasn't her controlling ex's behavior the sticking point in their relationship?

But part of her found it kind of hot for a guy to take charge every now and then. Besides, it wasn't like he was ordering her around. She knew without a doubt that if she'd declined the dress or the pajamas or the movie night, he would have backed down immediately. This take-charge side of Ben was what he'd hired her to help him tap into, right?

She slipped into the powder room he'd pointed to, amused by the notion that anyone could call it a "powder room." It was the size of her living room, complete with a sitting area and massive granite counter lined with two ornate copper sinks. Behind her was a row of shopping bags lined up on a velvet-cushioned bench. She peeked into the first and found several pairs of fuzzy pajama bottoms in various sizes and colors. The next bag held a few pairs of Lululemon yoga pants and some cute tops with built-in shelf bras.

He really did think of everything, she mused as she peeled off her dress and unhooked her bra, grateful to be free of the constricting garment. Of course, she doubted Ben had really been the one to think of the importance of getting rid of an underwire at the end of the day. More likely it had been his secretary who came up with the idea, but still. Just knowing he had a hand in helping her free the girls was enough to leave her feeling downright grateful.

She chose a pair of pale gray, rabbit-soft pajama bottoms that turned out to be cashmere, and a yellow cami top with a lined shelf bra that promised enough support to keep her decent in mixed company, but enough softness to let her breathe easy. A drapey lavender cardigan and a pair of fuzzy blue slippers completed the ensemble, and she padded back out into the living room feeling more comfortable than she'd felt in a long time.

Of course, she was still working, wasn't she? This was a job, after all. The lines were getting as fuzzy as the slippers on her feet. She'd certainly never had a job like this one, but she'd also never had a client like Ben.

Ben.

He was crouched on the living room floor fiddling with

the television, so he didn't see her come in. Behind him was a massive nest of blankets and two giant bowls of popcorn.

"Wow, you take movie night pretty seriously."

He looked up and grinned at her. "My dad has BALSAC, I have WoHaReHa."

"WoHaReHa? That sounds like a medical condition."

He laughed. "WoHaReHa—another acronym. Work Hard, Relax Harder."

"I didn't know you could relax hard."

"You can do anything hard if you put your mind to it." He grimaced. "Okay, that sounded dirtier than I meant it to."

Holly grinned and moved into the living room, settling into one corner of the blanket nest. She grabbed an orange bowl filled with popcorn and shoved a handful into her mouth. "Oh my God, real butter."

"Damn straight. It's the only way to eat popcorn. Can I get you something to drink?"

"I don't suppose you have root beer?"

"With or without ice cream?"

"I think I might love you."

He laughed and flicked something on the television, bringing the giant screen to life. He stood up and walked toward her, dropping the remote onto the blanket beside her. "I'll be right back."

He disappeared around the corner as Holly grabbed another handful of popcorn and thought about how nice this was. It wasn't normally how she'd behave with a brand new client, but there was nothing normal about this arrangement with Ben. Professionalism aside, there was something about him that made her feel like she'd known him for years. Like they were old college buddies or pals from middle school.

Of course, "buddy" and "pal" were the furthest words from her mind as he strode back into the room wearing navy fleece pants and a snug gray T-shirt. He was holding two root beer floats, and she couldn't decide which sight was more delicious.

"Here you go," he said, handing her one of the mugs. He shoved his glasses up his nose and sat down beside her, pulling a pile of blankets over his legs. There were at least three feet between them—a nice, platonic distance—but she could feel the warmth of his body even from this far away.

"What are we watching?" She took a sip of her root beer float, enjoying the creamy fizz on the back of her tongue.

"*Plan 9 from Outer Space.* Have you seen it?"

"I've never even heard of it."

"Excellent. It was made in 1959, and it's considered by many to be the worst movie ever made."

She gave a dry laugh. "And we're watching it *why*?"

He grinned and spooned up a bite of ice cream. "Because it's so bad, it's gloriously, tragically awful. You'll see." He dropped his spoon back in the mug, then picked up the remote and flicked a button.

He scrolled through a menu on the television screen as Holly snuggled back against the blankets and took a sip of her own float. It was creamy and delicious, with the perfect proportions of soda to ice cream. She watched the screen as the credits gave way to a grainy, black and white image of a funeral. She nibbled another handful of popcorn as the film segued into a parade of lurching zombies and flying saucers trailing along on strings.

"You weren't kidding," she said around a mouthful of root beer float. "This is terrible."

"I know." He grinned and reached into her popcorn bowl. "Isn't it awesome?"

"Kinda. Did you just steal my popcorn?"

"Mine's gone. You have plenty."

"Not if you keep snarfing it like that."

"Snarfing? Did you just make up a word?"

"I work in PR. If I can make an antisocial geek into a charming CEO, I can make a random string of sounds into a real word."

"Good point. Shh! This is the best part."

Holly smiled and grabbed another handful of popcorn, feeling ridiculously happy. It was more than just the delightful cheesiness of zombie attacks and bad acting. It was the closeness of Ben, the salty goodness of the popcorn, the cozy comfort of sharing a blanket nest with a big, strong man who looked like an oversized version of Clark Kent.

She kept stealing glimpses at him, marveling at the fact that she hadn't even known this guy twenty-four hours ago. She snuggled closer, telling herself it was just a friendly response to a friendly situation.

Ben glanced at her and shifted closer, near enough now that she could feel the heat from his bare arm. He plunged his hand into the popcorn at the precise moment she did the same, their greasy fingers tangling at the bottom of the bowl.

"Well this is awkward," he said, flashing her a grin that was anything but awkward. "Guess I should make more."

"Guess so."

"Or we could thumb wrestle for the last handful."

"Thumb wrestle?"

"Don't tell me you've never thumb wrestled?"

"Guilty as charged. Not only am I a *Plan 9* virgin, but also a thumb wrestling virgin."

He quirked an eyebrow at her, studying her face for a moment. Then he leaned closer, his breath ruffling her hair. "In that case, I believe it's my job to deflower you."

Chapter Six

Ben couldn't believe he was honestly trying to flirt with a gorgeous woman by using a bad sci-fi movie and a thumb wrestling challenge.

He also couldn't believe it was working.

"One, two, three, four, I declare a thumb war." He counted slowly, his fingers locked with Holly's as they moved their thumbs back and forth over each other in the bizarre digit dance that accompanied the rhyme. "Five, six, seven, eight, try to keep your thumb straight."

She giggled and lunged with her thumb, a valiant effort, but a misguided one. Her thumbs were half the length of his, and this was her first time playing. It was hardly a fair fight, but that didn't mean Ben planned to let go of her hand anytime soon.

"Oooh! Almost!" she cried as the pad of her thumb slid down the side of his, a gesture that shouldn't be sexy, but totally was. Her skin was warm, her hands were soft, and he could see straight down the front of her top to where she most definitely wasn't wearing a bra.

Of course, that was something his father would do, so Ben quickly looked away and focused on their intertwined fingers.

"Nice effort," he said, maneuvering his thumb to the side, letting her take another swipe at him. Her nails were polished with a tasteful shade of shell pink, and he had a crazy urge to suck the popcorn butter off one digit at a time.

Holly lunged again with her thumb, sitting up on her knees for a better angle. She was totally cheating, but he didn't care. He just wanted to keep touching her like this, to hear her laugh as she gripped his knuckles and maneuvered her thumb against his.

"Dammit! I almost had you." She laughed as he moved his thumb out from under hers without much effort. He let her get a little cockier, jabbing too quickly as he dodged easily out of her way.

"Nice try," he murmured. "Try keeping your hand steady."

"Like this?"

"Mmm-hmm. Better."

"Ha!" She attacked again. "You just wait, Mr. CEO. I will *own* you."

"I welcome the challenge."

Just like he welcomed the closeness of her body, warm and lush and round and so very, very near. Ben let her take another swipe at him, in no big hurry to end the game.

"I think you have an unfair advantage at thumb wrestling," Holly said as her thumb skittered off the side of his.

"How's that?"

"You have hands the size of baseball mitts. Seriously, did you eat your Wheaties as a kid or what?"

"Something like that."

She grinned and pounced again, her thumb sliding off his and making everything jiggle pleasantly beneath that pale yellow top. He should probably stop it—both the game and his urge to ogle her. It was hardly the right tone to set for the

CEO of a major corporation and the branding expert he'd hired to turn him into a suave, sophisticated leader.

"Oh, you are so dead!" She laughed again, and Ben decided suave and sophisticated were overrated.

He hooked the pad of his thumb over the top of her nail, pressing it firm against the top of their locked fingers. "One," he counted, slow enough to let her squirm away if she wanted. "Two—"

"Ha!" she declared, wriggling free in an impressive display of agility. "Not so fast, big guy."

"Still primed for battle, I see?"

"Battle, yes! I feel like we should have body armor or maybe swords."

"I'll see if my assistant can run to the Thumb Wrestling Emporium before our next tournament."

She took another stab at pinning him, and Ben let her press his thumb down for a good three seconds before he slid out from under her. His father would roll his eyes if he saw this. It was hardly the most professional activity, certainly not something his father or any of the other suits at that party would be doing on a quiet Tuesday night.

But hadn't his dad always encouraged competition and athletic pursuits as a platform for professional networking?

This probably isn't what he meant.

"Ready for me to put you out of your misery?" Ben flexed his thumb dramatically and flashed Holly a grin he hoped made his words sound less cocky.

But hell, she was training him to be confident in business dealings. Wasn't this good practice?

"I'd like to see you try," she taunted.

"Very well." He slid his thumb over hers and clamped down, pinning her digit with relative ease. Her eyes widened, and he felt her wriggling beneath him, trying to get free.

"Hey!" She giggled and tried to pull back, but Ben held

tight.

"One, two, three, four, it appears I've won this thumb war." He held her gaze for a moment, smiling with triumph and maybe a little lust. Then he let go of her hand and took off his glasses. He lifted the hem of his shirt and used it to wipe a smudge off one of the lenses. "I believe I've made my point."

Holly drew her hand back, though Ben was pleased to see she didn't put any distance between them. "What point is that?"

"Nerds can be fierce and valiant in combat."

"Nerds can also have six-pack abs, apparently." She reached out and patted his bare midsection, and Ben dropped his shirt hem and stopped polishing his glasses. "Between those and the monster paws, you're unlike any nerd I've ever met."

"Monster paws?"

"Big hands, big feet—monster paws."

"I'll have to have that printed on my business cards."

She grinned and reached for his hand again. "Come on, best two out of three?"

"You want to thumb wrestle again?"

"Afraid you'll lose?"

Ben set his glasses aside and turned back to her. She'd gotten one thing right—he was no dummy. If she was offering him the opportunity to touch her again in any capacity, he was sure as hell going to take it.

He locked his fingers with hers again and stared into her eyes. "You sure about this?"

She held his gaze, not moving, not blinking, not even smiling now. Then she nodded slowly, making no move to initiate the game. "Positive."

"Ready?"

"Uh-huh. Let's do this."

His gaze was still locked with hers, and he could see her

chest rising and falling at a quicker rate than it had been a few seconds ago. He wasn't the best with social cues, but something told him she wasn't talking about thumb wrestling anymore.

"You know…" she said softly. "This is actually even more impressive than your abs."

"What's that?"

"I've been here less than an hour and you've already got me braless and tangled up in your bedding while we hold hands."

Ben felt the blood drain from his brain and head south. He held tight to her hand. "Technically, you're the one who took your bra off."

"Even more impressive. You got me to do the hard work. Clearly the mark of a strategic-thinking, alpha male businessman."

"So what would a strategic-thinking, alpha male businessman do next to demonstrate his budding leadership skills?"

Her throat moved as she swallowed, and something that looked a little like fear flashed in her eyes. Then it was gone, replaced by something he thought might be lust. Had he really inspired that?

"I suppose he might take the initiative to kiss me," she said softly.

"You think so?"

"Don't we owe it to your professional development to give it a shot?"

Her tone was teasing, but there was something else there. A challenge or an invitation. He wasn't quite sure, but one thing he did know—he desperately wanted to kiss her, had been thinking about it every minute since he first touched his lips to hers in the furniture store.

He let go of her hand and slid his fingers over the nape

of her neck, moving slowly, giving her the chance to say no if she wanted to.

"Yes," she murmured, and she surged forward, knocking him backward onto the sea of blankets as her lips found his. She kissed him hard, then drew back, grinning on top of him. "And that's how you pin someone in thumb wrestling."

"I'm glad my uncle never played like that." He drew her mouth to his again, then rolled her over, pinning her beneath him on a fluffy blue down-filled comforter. He deepened the kiss and she responded in kind, soft and sweet and hungry. Her body arched against his as her thighs wrapped around him, holding him against her. He could feel the warmth between her legs and wondered if she'd ditched the panties when she changed in the bathroom. The thought made him hard. *Harder.* God, she felt good.

Holly moaned and pressed her body tighter against his as Ben skimmed a palm down her arm, feeling goose bumps rise on her flesh. He kept kissing her, pretty sure he never wanted to stop. Something about this reminded him of a high school make-out session, though he couldn't honestly say why. Graduating from high school at sixteen meant he'd missed out on a lot of those milestones, but he wasn't missing a damn thing now. She felt warm and soft beneath him, and her whole body was molded against his.

Ben broke the kiss to plant another one behind her ear, then down her throat and over her collarbone. Holly moaned as he slid lower, lifting the hem of her shirt to make a trail of kisses down her rib cage, over her belly, then up again.

"God, that feels good."

"Mmm," he murmured, pushing aside the elastic inside the shirt. He wasn't sure if it was there to hold her breasts in place or to deter unwanted groping, but the way she was writhing and gasping beneath him told Ben none of this was unwanted.

His mouth found her nipple—

She gasped and threaded her fingers into his hair. "Don't stop."

"Wouldn't dream of it."

He took his time on her breasts, licking, sucking, dipping into the hollow between them and resurfacing on the other side to give the same attention to the other one. By the time he came up for air, Holly was panting like she'd just run a marathon. She pressed a hand to his chest, then pushed him away.

Ben started to apologize, but she got to her knees and pulled off her top. She flung it across the room as he sat up too, putting them face to face. She reached for him again as he slid his hands up her sides to cup one breast in each hand.

"You have the best hands," she moaned, pressing so hard against them he thought he might hurt her. He squeezed softly, making her groan again, and he marveled at the notion that he could rouse such a response in her. Her breasts were perfectly sized, not too big and not too small, just the right fit in the center of his palms.

He found her lips again and kissed her, breathing in the scent of flowers and buttered popcorn. Holly moved against him as he slid his thumbs over her nipples again just to hear her gasp. He felt her fingers clutching at the hem of his shirt, and he let her pull it up and over his head so they were skin on skin. She felt so fucking good, so soft and warm and pliant against him.

Her fingers clenched around his biceps, and he let her pull him back down to the ground beside her. Lying on his left side next to her, he let his right hand move down her abdomen, his fingers dipping under the waistband of the gray cashmere pants. He went slow, giving her a chance to say no or remind him this wasn't a good way to establish a business relationship.

Instead, she raised her hips so he could slide her pants

the rest of the way off. Christ, he couldn't believe this was happening, but he seemed powerless to stop it. His fingers trailed between her legs as she opened them wider.

"God you're wet," he murmured.

"I swear I don't usually do this with someone I've just—"

"Shhh," he murmured, kissing her to halt any explanation she felt she might need to deliver.

He wasn't interested in judging her. He was interested in tasting her.

He slid down her body, leaving a wet trail of kisses as he went. First her belly button, then her hipbone, then the crease of her leg, then—

"Oh my God!"

Her fingers gripped his head as his tongue probed her center, tasting, teasing, circling. Holly arched her back and clutched his hair as his tongue made slow circles around her clit. God, she tasted amazing. He shifted his weight to one elbow, freeing his right hand to move between her thighs. He slid one finger in, making her gasp again as he circled his tongue faster, working the sensitive nub.

He let his finger glide in and out, feeling her press against him with each stroke. She tensed around him, and he flattened his tongue, wanting her to feel him everywhere.

"I'm close," she gasped, and the words sent a jolt through him.

He could feel her coiled like a spring beneath him as he licked her again. It was a powerful feeling, knowing all he had to do was slide his finger in again, stroke her just once more with his tongue and then—

"Ben!" she screamed and dug her nails into his shoulders, bucking against him. He was delirious with the taste of her and the tight clench of her body around him. She screamed again, and he dropped one hand to her hip to hold her steady as he licked and stroked and sucked until he felt her go slack beneath him.

Ben drew back and rested a hand on her belly. She was lying back on the comforter with her eyes closed. Her cheeks were flushed and damp and a strand of dark hair lay plastered to her cheek. Ben had never seen anything so beautiful in his entire life, and he wanted her all over again.

Holly opened her eyes and smiled. "Holy cow. That was amazing."

Ben grinned. "Science geeks study a lot of human anatomy."

She laughed. "Was that the secret? I thought it might be the monster paws."

"That too."

"Seriously, you could teach classes. How'd you get so good at that?"

He planted a kiss on her hipbone, tamping down the urge to feel cocky. "Uh, not to get too clinical, but there's a distinct advantage to long fingers and a good angle."

Holly laughed and sat up, brushing her hair from her cheek. "So that's a G-spot, huh? And I thought I was the one here to teach you the lessons."

Ben watched a crinkle form between her brows as she played her own words back to herself in her mind. Apparently, she didn't like the way they sounded, because she sat up a little straighter and reached for her shirt.

"Look, I guess I should have thought of this before we got too carried away, but this probably isn't a good idea."

"You mean for me to write you a check and then have you end up naked on my living room floor?"

She grimaced. "Ouch."

"Sorry," he said, wishing he hadn't tried to be flip. "I didn't mean to make it sound like prostitution."

"No, I'm sorry. I feel like I should reciprocate here, and God knows I really, *really* want to—" She shot a look at his crotch. "Really." He watched her throat move as she swallowed hard. Then she turned and yanked her shirt on. "I feel like I shouldn't take your money now." She pulled on her pants, her fingers fumbling with the drawstring. "This whole thing is a little unethical, but you're right—it's the money changing hands that makes it really bad."

"Look, I was just joking. There's no reason this should interfere with our professional relationship."

"That's just it. I can't go sleeping with a client. That's like the most unprofessional move in the book."

"Technically, we didn't sleep together."

She rolled her eyes as she cinched the waistband of the cashmere pants, and Ben tried not to take the double knot personally.

"Okay then, we didn't sleep together, we had sex," she said. "Let's not get hung up on semantics."

"I'm not faulting your word choice. Just observing that no sexual intercourse took place. I went down on you, you came, end of story."

The flush in her cheeks told him the story was far from over, and Ben was inclined to agree. Still, he pressed on. "Look, we can still maintain a professional relationship here."

"Ben—"

"Please, Holly. I need you. Having you there coaching me through the event tonight was a godsend. I can't do this CEO thing without you. Not yet, anyway. I still have a lot of work to do before I'm fit to fill my father's shoes."

She frowned, which Ben felt like doing, too, as his own words echoed in his ears. The last thing he wanted was to be his father, but that's exactly what he was counting on Holly to help him do.

If you're trying not to emulate the worst of your dad, hooking up with a woman you hired is probably not the best move.

Dammit. Okay, he could still fix this.

"Look, I can be good," he said.

"No kidding." A ghost of a smile crossed her features, but she bit her lip and dropped her gaze. "Sorry, not helpful. Also, I'm really sorry about leaving you high and dry. If you want, I could—" Her voice trailed off, but he caught her meaning as her gaze shifted to his crotch.

"It's okay. You're right, we should keep things professional between us. Please—let's give it a shot."

She looked down into her lap and fiddled with the tie on the front of the cashmere pants. "No more fooling around?"

"Scout's honor," he said, raising his hand with his palm toward her, thumb extended, fingers parted between his middle and ring finger.

Holly stared at his hand and frowned. "What the hell kind of Boy Scout were you?"

"I wasn't. That's a Vulcan salute."

"*Star Trek*?"

"Yep. Much more meaningful to a geek than any Boy Scout pledge. As Spock is my witness, I'll do my very best to keep my hands off you."

She stared at his hand a few beats, and he wondered if she was pondering the magnitude of his geekiness or remembering how his fingers had felt sliding in and out of her.

At last she raised her hand, moving her fingers into her own version of the Vulcan salute. "Well okay then," she said. "Live long and prosper and grope no more."

•••

"You slept with him?" Miriam raised her palm in a gesture Holly wished didn't leave her thinking salacious thoughts about Ben's monster paws and his Vulcan salute. "Come on," Miriam urged, waving her hand in Holly's face and jingling the gold bracelet on her wrist. "This calls for a high five."

"I'm not high-fiving you," Holly whispered, glancing toward the conference room door. She'd had it soundproofed when she and Miriam first took over the space and had it built out to their specifications, back when they were just starting out with First Impressions. Even so, she didn't want to take any chances. "Besides, as Ben pointed out—we didn't technically sleep together."

"That's right, he follows the Bill Clinton definition of sex." Miriam waved her un-high-fived palm dismissively and grinned at Holly. "Come on, this is a big deal."

"It's not a big deal, and it's not happening again," Holly said, pretty sure she meant it. "Come on, we can't go knocking boots with our clients any old time we feel like it."

"We own the company, hon." Miriam scooped up a spoonful of Greek yogurt while Holly took a nervous sip of her iced tea. "We can pretty much make the rules."

"Right. And I think the rules of professional conduct are pretty clear on the fact that it's a bad idea to get romantically involved with someone who's paying you to rebrand his corporate identity."

"I'm pretty sure there are no rules for that particular arrangement," Miriam pointed out. "Didn't you kinda make up that whole thing? It's not like there's a user manual for rebranding a *person*."

Holly sighed. "Hooking up with a client would be bad under the best of circumstances. Hooking up with the one client whose fee is going to get us out of this mess with the bank is just idiotic. I don't want to blow this."

"You didn't blow anything, which is kinda too bad for Ben." Miriam grinned. "That was very generous of him."

"You're impossible." Holly forked up a bite of her salad, not sure if guilt or lust was winning out in her carousel of moods this morning. Part of her wanted to be ashamed of herself and committed to never, ever getting intimate with a client.

Part of her just wanted Ben's hands on her body again.

Stop it. Remember what happened the last time you let a guy wedge himself in the middle of your career?

"You just made a face like you want to stab something besides that cherry tomato," Miriam said around a bite of yogurt. "What are you thinking?"

"About Chase," she admitted.

"Ew. Can we not talk about your ex when I'm eating?"

"Well you were the one who asked."

"Fair point." Miriam poked her spoon into the yogurt again. "Why are you thinking about Chase when you're still wearing that morning-after glow from your evening with Ben?"

Holly sighed. "Because fooling around with a career-obsessed guy is how I got into trouble last time, remember?"

"You think I might have forgotten the dickhead whose name is still on our damn mortgage and who ordered you to quit working and squeeze out his babies?" Miriam shook her head. "Not all guys are like that, Holly. Some even believe in the novel concept that women can have careers *and* husbands *and* families. Imagine that."

"We're getting off track here," Holly said, wishing Miriam's words didn't sting so much. "Right now it's the career I need to focus on, and the fact that this job with Ben is going to help us get my asshole ex off the loan."

"Fine. At least tell me if Ben was good."

Holly felt her face grow hot. "I don't kiss and tell."

Miriam gave her a smug look and licked the back of her spoon. "From what you told me, he did a lot more of the kissing than you did. For the record, there's nothing hotter than a guy who's eager to go downtown. Didn't you tell me once that Chase was so averse to chowing box you practically had to grab him by the ears and push his head between your legs?"

"God, I can't believe I told you that. Or any of it, really. I just needed someone to talk to about it."

"As your best friend and business partner, you won't get any judgment from me. My lips are sealed. Which is more than I can say for yours." She grinned wider, and Holly wished the ground would swallow her up.

"Miriam—"

"Okay, okay, I'll stop teasing you. I do want to point out that you didn't do anything wrong. You're both consenting adults, right?"

"Right."

If by *consenting,* she meant tearing off her clothes and spreading her legs and begging Ben to put his mouth on her within twelve hours of meeting him. God, what did he think of her? She'd left in a hurry last night, barely remembering to grab her shoes or purse or the loungewear Ben insisted she take with her.

"I'll call you tomorrow," he'd shouted after her as she ran for the elevator like the building was on fire.

Now, Holly glanced at her phone and tried not to notice it was already after two. She'd stayed busy all day, working straight through lunch and resisting the urge to call or text Ben. Though she was still on the fence about whether continuing their professional relationship was a good idea, she'd created a detailed rebranding plan for him. Watching him in action last night—at the event, not on the living room floor—had given her plenty of ideas where Ben could stand to improve his skills.

There was no need for improvement of any kind with his skills on the living room floor.

She'd worked up a detailed SWOT analysis, identifying strengths, weaknesses, opportunities, and threats based on her own observations at the event, and on the spreadsheet of information Ben had sent yesterday afternoon. She had a lot to offer him. She could do a lot of good with this assignment, proving to herself and to Ben that she was good at her job. That she took her career seriously.

Chase sure as hell never did.

"Did you have a chance to look at the RFP from Urban Trax?" Miriam asked.

Holly turned her attention back to Miriam, grateful to be talking about business again. At least that was a comforting topic. "Urban Trax," she repeated. "That's the chain of outdoor stores?"

"Yes, kinda like REI."

"Sorry, I've been a little out of the loop with that one."

"Don't sweat it, I have things covered. Here, check out the preliminary logos I was brainstorming last night."

Miriam swiped the screen on her iPad and brought up a PDF featuring several impressive mock-ups. She handed the device to Holly, and Holly scrolled through the sample logos, amazed once again at the caliber of talent on the First Impressions team.

"Wow, this one's amazing."

"Thanks," Miriam said. "That's my favorite, too. It's a little premature until we land the deal, but I'm confident we will."

"Keep me posted," Holly said, forking up another bite of salad. "I should have an update on the Happy Valley account by the end of the day."

"No rush. I know this Langley Enterprises job is kind of a priority right now."

Holly nodded, conscious of the heat that spread through her body at the thought of Ben and his company. "Yeah, it is. It's not just about the CEO rebranding, either."

"You think there's potential for more work?"

"I'm hoping. It's a big opportunity."

"Exactly how big are we talking?"

Holly's thoughts veered to images of Ben's massive hands, his broad shoulders, the impressive bulge she'd felt in the front of his pants—

"Earth to Holly?"

"Sorry," she said, dabbing her mouth with a napkin. "I was just thinking about our prospects for new business."

"You were thinking about your prospects for getting in the CEO's pants," Miriam said, flashing a salacious grin. "I know you, girl. I can read it all over your face."

"Right," Holly said, wondering if working with your best friend was almost as dangerous as sleeping with a client. "Anyway, I do think First Impressions could end up with a lot of business out of this Langley deal. They have corporate offices all over the world, and a budget big enough to make your head spin."

"Does each division handle their own marketing?"

"It all runs through corporate headquarters, but individual branches have budgets for promotional initiatives and marketing campaigns. Ben sent me a little info about it yesterday, and I couldn't believe the numbers. If we could get a piece of that—"

She stopped short, waiting for Miriam to point out that she'd already gotten a piece. When she didn't, it occurred to her that her potty-mouthed pal wasn't the only one with sex on the brain.

"Anyway," Holly said. "If things go well with this CEO rebrand, maybe there's potential for First Impressions to do some work for other Langley divisions."

All the more reason not to bone your client, her inner voice pointed out. *You don't want to screw that up by screwing the CEO.*

"Sounds good," Miriam said, tucking a crumpled napkin and an apple core into her empty yogurt container as she stood up. "I have to run to that meeting for Mountain Medical Group. You want to chat later about the bid for that cable company?"

"Let's aim for tomorrow. My calendar's up to date, so just pick a time that works."

"Sounds like a plan." Miriam squeezed her shoulder. "Now get out there and bone that CEO."

"I will do no such thing."

"Whatever you say."

As Miriam walked away, Holly crumpled her napkin onto her salad plate and sighed.

She felt confident in her ability to juggle multiple clients and to run this business the way she'd been doing the last couple years. She even felt confident in her ability to rebrand Ben Langley into the sort of alpha male CEO he needed to be.

If only she felt half as confident in her ability to resist him.

Chapter Seven

Ben glanced at his watch for what had to be the hundredth time in the last hour. When he'd emailed Holly the previous afternoon to request a two o'clock meeting the next day, he hadn't considered the fact that having thirty-six hours pass before seeing her again would feel like an eternity.

It's strictly business.

Except his brain kept veering to images of her naked and breathless on his living room floor. Maybe this was supposed to be strictly business, but there was a lot more than business on his mind.

He glanced at his watch again. Two minutes until she was due to arrive.

"Dude!"

Ben looked up to see Parker standing in the doorway shaking his head. His best friend wore athletic shorts, a T-shirt from their boxing gym, and a look of intense annoyance.

"You stood us up again." Parker ambled forward and dropped into the seat Ben had hoped to see cupping Holly's firm backside in mere seconds.

"Shit, I'm sorry," Ben said. "I'm working around the clock on this new deal and—"

"And becoming your dad with every passing day. Nice suit."

Ben sighed. "I'm sorry. Seriously, I'd love nothing more than to hit the gym with you guys, but this job is important."

"You're aware the rest of us have jobs, too, right? Some of our titles even include words like 'president' and 'chief executive.'"

"You're clearly a better man than I am."

Parker shook his head. "Wow, the stress is really getting to you. Did your dad have your sense of humor surgically removed before he granted you a key to the building?"

"Sorry." Ben raked his hands through his hair. "It's just—this is my shot, you know? To take the company in a new direction and make up for some of the shit my dad pulled when my mom was still alive."

"That's an awful lot of weight to put on your shoulders."

Ben shrugged. "It is what it is."

"Fine. We'll cut you some slack for now, but if you start growing ear hair and slapping people on the back like your dad, we're hosting an intervention." Parker grinned. "It'll be like that time in college when you wanted to go to that insect convention and we had to kidnap you so you'd come with us for spring break in Cancun."

"And I missed out on seeing a rare Dryococelus Australis."

"Yeah, but the margaritas were outstanding."

"I did have a good time," Ben admitted, glancing at his watch again. "Speaking of time, I have an important meeting starting any second now."

As if on cue, the intercom buzzed on his desk. "Holly Colvin is here to see you?"

Parker raised an eyebrow, and Ben tried to ignore him. "Thanks, Carol," he said. "You can send her in."

He looked at Parker, who was shooting him a knowing

grin. "What?" Ben asked. "My meeting happens to be with a woman."

"Who happens to make you grin like you just won a gift certificate from the blowjob-of-the-month club."

"Very nice. You can go now."

Parker stood up just as Holly strode through the door looking flushed and beautiful in a slim skirt with a crisp green blouse that looked like it would be silky to touch.

Stop thinking about touching her.

Ben stood up and stepped around his desk to greet her. "Holly," he said, extending his hand. He realized belatedly that offering a handshake to a woman he'd seen naked thirty-six hours ago was the most socially awkward greeting he could have managed, but she met him with a firm grip and a smile.

"Ben. Good to see you again." Her gaze drifted to Parker, and Ben realized he should probably introduce his oldest pal instead of standing there like an idiot.

"This is Parker," he offered. "He was just leaving."

"No I wasn't," Parker said, extending a hand to Holly. "You'll have to excuse my friend. He's completely devoid of charm and social skill."

"Which is precisely why Holly's here," Ben said. "That's top secret, by the way. You say a word to my dad and I'll beat you to death with my paperweight."

Parker smiled at Holly with renewed interest. "You're his life coach?"

"I never said life coach," Ben reminded him. "Holly owns a PR and branding firm. She's going to rebrand me into a polished, professional CEO."

Parker laughed and leaned against the doorframe looking amused. "I hope you charged double. You've got your work cut out for you with this one."

Holly smiled at Parker, and Ben tried not to notice the faint burn of jealousy flaring in his gut. "How do you mean?" she asked, glancing from Parker to Ben. "This could actually be pretty helpful to the process, you know—hearing firsthand from your closest friends where your strengths and weaknesses lie."

"Oh, don't even get me started on Ben's weaknesses." Parker grinned and shot Ben a look he recognized as a subtle request for permission. Parker might joke, but he wasn't the sort of guy to throw his buddy under the bus.

Ben just shrugged. Parker was right that Holly had her work cut out for her, so she might as well know what she was dealing with.

"Let's see," Parker said, pretending to ponder. "There's the time Ben tried to pick up a woman by offering to defrag her hard drive."

"She slapped me, if I remember right," Ben mused.

"Well, it does sound kinda dirty," Holly pointed out.

"Then there's the time a couple years ago when none of us had seen him for a week," Parker said, getting comfortable now. "We went down to the engineering lab and found out he'd been working for ten days straight on some new chemical breakthrough or something. He'd been taking sponge baths in the bathroom sink and eating nothing but carrot sticks and Cool Ranch Doritos."

"They were Salsa Verde Doritos," Ben said.

"My mistake." Parker scratched his chin. "Or how about the time we finally persuaded him to take a break and treat himself to a Hawaii vacation."

"That sounds nice," Holly said, and Ben couldn't help picturing her in a bikini frolicking on the sand.

"Sure it does," Parker agreed. "Only instead of taking surfing lessons and drinking mai-tais on the beach, Ben spent the whole trip studying the flora and fauna of the islands."

"I wonder if I still have that research paper. I discovered a new species of fungus." Ben glanced at Holly, wondering if she was second-guessing her decision to take him on or take off her bra in his house. She smiled at him, and Ben felt his heart dissolve in his chest.

"Ben's the best guy I know, though," Parker said. "He'd throw himself in front of a train to save anyone he loves."

"That doesn't sound very sensible," Ben said. "The average velocity of a locomotive is—"

"Shut up, brainiac—I'm trying to sing your praises here." Parker turned back to Holly. "I met Ben our first year in grad school. I was twenty-three, but Ben was only nineteen. The dude went to college at sixteen and finished in less than three years. Anyway, one night we hooked him up with a fake ID and dragged him out barhopping with us. Sure enough, Ben got busted."

"What?" Holly looked at him. "You got arrested?"

Ben quirked an eyebrow at her. "That surprises you?"

"Kinda." She turned back to Parker. "So what happened?"

"The cops were doing this big sting operation trying to break up this ring of guys producing fake IDs. They offered to let Ben go if he told them where he got it, but Ben refused to turn in his friends. Wouldn't give them any names, not even when they held him in jail for three days and made him miss a test that could screw up his whole GPA."

"Wow."

Parker laughed. "I finally went in there and turned *myself* in so the dumbass wouldn't rot in jail forever. But he would have, if it had come to it. The guy's loyal to a fault."

Holly was giving him an appraising look, which made Ben uncomfortable. He wasn't used to being the center of attention, which was probably one more thing he'd need to overcome if he wanted to be a CEO. God, the list was getting long.

"Sounds like you're giving me some nice raw material to work with," she said. "I'm eager to get started."

"Have fun with that," Parker told her, then turned to Ben. "I've gotta go, but I'll see you at the gym tomorrow?"

"I'll do my best," Ben said.

"Later," Parker called, heading out the door. "Take good care of him, Holly."

"I plan to," she murmured as she pulled the door closed and turned back to Ben. "That was enlightening."

"I'm glad you thought so. Have a seat."

She seemed to hesitate, then sat down on the opposite side of the desk and folded her hands in her lap. "So have you had a chance to look over the rebranding plan I sent over yesterday?"

"I did. You really think we can cover all those bases in time for the presentation?"

"I think so. It might mean a few late nights here and there, but—" She bit her lip, and Ben watched the tips of her ears turn pink. "I didn't mean it like that."

"Like what?"

"Late nights and—never mind." She sighed. "Look, I have to level with you, Ben. This feels awkward."

"How do you mean?"

"You're a smart guy. Is that a real question?"

"Not really," he admitted, grinning. "I just wanted to hear you say it."

"Fine. I'll say it. Having you make me come my brains out was mind-blowing, and I haven't stopped thinking about it. But that's the problem."

"How is that a problem?" he asked, trying not to gloat.

"Because I need to be focusing on how to make you a better CEO. You hired me to do a job, and it behooves us both to stay focused on the task."

"What about the point you made about unleashing my inner 'strategic-thinking, alpha male businessman?'" he asked, and watched her flush again. "I think what happened between us was very helpful toward that goal."

"Right. I can't argue with that. You definitely showed

some—initiative."

Ben rested his palms on the desk and watched Holly's blush deepen as her gaze dropped to his hands. "Initiative," he said. "Is that what the kids are calling it these days?"

"Ben, seriously—"

"Hey, I'm just reminding you what you said about me needing to become a take-charge sort of guy." He grinned, reveling in the chance to banter like this. It wasn't often he voiced his thoughts so clearly. Holly was a good influence in more ways than one. "The bedroom's a pretty good place to practice. Or the living room floor. Or up against a kitchen counter. Or—"

"I don't disagree, Ben," she said, clearing her throat. "And yeah, I enjoyed it. *A lot.* But I'm here to do a job." She held up a hand. "And before you say it, I'm not talking about hand jobs or blowjobs."

He laughed. "I wasn't going to go there, but now that you have—"

"My career is important to me," she said. "Handling this rebranding process effectively and professionally is important to me. You can understand that, can't you?"

"I can," he admitted, trying not to be too disappointed at the prospect of being thrown over for her job. He had to respect her position, even if he wished he could explore a lot of other positions with her.

Crap, he had to stop thinking like that. Maybe he was going a little too far with this alpha male thing.

"I understand," he said at last. "This is important to me, too. I know we both need to focus our full attention on it."

"I'm glad we cleared that up."

"Me, too," Ben said, not feeling so glad. "So do you want to review the plan?"

She smiled, then nodded. "Let's get to work."

Chapter Eight

"Ben, my boy!"

He tried not to grit his teeth as his dad marched into his office without knocking, interrupting him for what had to be the hundredth time that day.

Ben pasted on his most cheerful grin, remembering Holly's suggestion that he make eye contact and think about something that made him happy so his smile reached his eyes even when the rest of him felt like yawning or screaming in frustration.

His brain locked onto an image of Holly spread naked and warm on his living room floor, and he found himself smiling a lot wider than he wanted to. He forced himself to dial it back a notch, pretty sure that wasn't the image he needed in his brain while he was dealing with his dad.

"What can I do for you, Dad?"

"Well, son, it looks like things are getting serious with the Kleinberger account."

"Wow, that's great." Ben picked up a fountain pen from the corner of his desk, not sure if he intended to take notes or just needed something to do with his hands. "I thought Kleinberger wasn't planning to make a decision until the end of the month."

"That was the plan, but they're speeding things along. Apparently, they got their budget pushed through a little earlier than they expected, so they want to get a jump on things. I told 'em you'd be happy to throw together a special presentation for them. You know, do a little razzle-dazzle for the execs who haven't seen what we're about yet."

"Me?" Ben swallowed, hating the petulance in his voice almost as much as he hated the thought of taking on yet another schmoozy project when his desk was overflowing with spreadsheets and business plans. He cleared his throat and tried again. "Obviously, I planned to be involved with the presentation, but I wasn't expecting to deliver it. Besides, I thought it wasn't happening until the end of the month."

Lyle frowned. "Well, things have changed, and you need a chance to demonstrate your oral presentation skills."

"I've been working on my oral presentation skills," he said, his mind straying to thoughts of burying his face between Holly's thighs. "And honing my skills as a strategic-thinking, alpha male businessman."

His dad looked at him like he'd just spoken Swahili, and Ben figured it was best if he refrained from admitting just how he'd been honing his skills.

"I know I usually take the lead on the sales side of things, but it's time you start stepping up and getting your feet wet." Lyle folded his arms over his chest. "You need to take on a more active role when it comes to the sales side of the job. You know, really get in there and make yourself familiar with the showmanship aspect of this company's leadership." Lyle frowned again. "Also, they might have asked for you."

"What?"

Lyle's scowl deepened. "Yes. Well, apparently the

Kleinberger execs enjoyed talking with you the other night at the event. They thought your no-nonsense, numbers-driven approach was 'refreshing,' and they wanted you to do the presentation so you could answer some of their questions about all the numbers and science mumbo jumbo."

Lyle had put "refreshing" in air quotes that made it clear exactly what he thought of the company's choice to request Ben for the presentation. Still, it was a vote of confidence that felt pretty good. A sign that his plan to steer Langley into the next generation of business wasn't so far off the mark.

"I'm flattered," Ben said. "And honored."

And terrified. And a little sick to my stomach.

"So can you pull this off?" his dad asked.

"How soon?"

"Friday afternoon. The agenda's already been circulated. You just have to show up and give the spiel, then work your magic. You know, turn on the ol' charm."

"Charm," Ben repeated, trying not to feel glum. "I'll see what I can do."

Lyle grinned and elbowed Ben in the ribs. "Too bad you can't bring that new girlfriend of yours. She seems like she could charm the pants off just about anyone."

"Holly?"

"Yeah, was that her name? Cute little gal. Not as busty as I like 'em, but great legs."

Ben felt his blood pressure starting to rise, but he held his temper in check and picked up his letter opener. "She's a very intelligent and accomplished woman," Ben said.

"I'm sure she is."

"I admire her intellect and business acumen."

"Of course you do. Is that how you ended up with her lipstick all over your fly the other night?"

Ben gripped his pen a little tighter, trying to come up with a response that sounded more believable than a story of a broken zipper in the dressing room. He was still working on it when his dad laughed and elbowed him again.

"Be there on Friday. I'll tell the boys at Kleinberger to expect you at eleven."

With that, Lyle marched out of the room, leaving Ben with the sinking feeling that this was all happening much too fast.

The presentation, or your relationship with Holly?

He shook his head, reminding himself there was no relationship. It was purely professional.

What part of geeky movies, thumb wrestling, and oral sex did you find professional?

Okay, fine. He might have crossed the line with Holly the other night. A few lines, really. His brain flooded with the memory of her spread open on his living room floor, warm and willing and gasping with pleasure. Pleasure *he'd* been the one to deliver. The memory of it made him feel a lot more accomplished than any deal with Kleinberger could.

Focus.

He reached for the phone and dialed Holly's number. He knew from her bio that she had extensive experience in public speaking. She did media training for corporate executives, and even created podcasts on how to give effective public presentations. She was the right woman for the job, period.

Never mind that he couldn't stop thinking about her, or that he desperately, urgently wanted to see her again and—

"Hello?"

"Hey, Holly, it's Ben. Langley? Of Langley Ent—"

"Hi, Ben. Of course, it's good to hear from you again."

Christ, why were they talking to each other like strangers? He knew what kind of panties she wore and how she made this soft little mewling sound right before she came.

Don't think about that, don't think about that, don't think about—

"Listen, Holly. You know that Kleinberger presentation I told you about?"

"Of course."

"The timeline just changed, and so did my role in it."

"How do you mean?"

"Instead of just preparing the presentation, I now have to give it. As in public speaking. Not my favorite thing."

"Ah," she said, her voice warm and soothing. "Did you know that for most people, a fear of public speaking ranks above fear of death, spiders, heights, and confined spaces?"

"So you're saying most people would rather be trapped in a casket full of spiders and hoisted onto a rooftop than give this presentation I just got asked to deliver?"

Holly laughed, and Ben pictured the soft dimple in her right cheek, the one that only appeared when she smiled really wide. He loved that damn dimple.

"So tell me about this presentation," she said, clearing her throat. "What's the topic?"

"Razzle-dazzle, apparently. I'm not sure if I'm supposed to throw glitter or juggle sparklers."

"Let's save those for the end of the presentation. Is there a topic?"

"The main focus is on some new products we manufacture that would be perfect for this client."

"You have data to back that up?"

"Of course. It's not the material I'm hung up on. It's the pizazz. The schmooze. The passionate delivery. None of that is my forte."

"Oh, I don't know about that. I think you've got passionate delivery nailed."

Ben blinked, surprised by her boldness. Apparently, Holly was surprised, too, since the next words out of her mouth were a stammered jumble of syllables.

"I, uh—I didn't—I mean, that came out wrong. I meant

the other night."

"Right," Ben said as he felt a slow smile creep across his face.

"At the event," she said, rushing her words together. "I heard you talking with the VP of human resources about your proposal to donate a portion of the company's proceeds to the American Cancer Society, and you sounded very passionate about that. And about Langley's bioengineering division. And about bad sci-fi movies. You were very passionate about all that."

Ben pictured her sitting at her desk with her dark hair pinned on top of her head and her odd lavender-gray eyes darting around as she tried to regain her professional composure. He should probably throw her a rope, but listening to her fumble was almost as endearing as knowing damn well she'd been thinking about the other night as much as he had.

"I'm passionate about some things," Ben said. "The things that matter. The things that give me a good reason to perfect my technique."

"Right. Um, when did you want to meet? I have an opening next Monday around three."

"Yeah, see, that's the problem. They moved up the timeline."

"How soon?"

"The presentation is Friday."

"Wow. Okay—um, how much public speaking have you done?"

"Do you want to count the acceptance speech I gave when I won the national chess tournament at age eight?"

"Sure."

"Then once."

"Oh." She was quiet a moment, and Ben wondered if she was consulting her schedule or pondering the magnitude of his geekery. Maybe both.

She cleared her throat. "Okay, if I reschedule my four o'clock and skip out on tonight's team dinner—"

"I don't want you to miss a team dinner on account of me."

"No, it's fine. Miriam—that's my business partner—she and I take turns running them each month. This one is hers anyway."

"Okay then. Do you want to come to my place?"

"No!" She couldn't have sounded more alarmed if he'd asked her to go nude skydiving as an exercise in assertiveness. She must have recognized it, too, because she softened her voice. "I mean—I think it would be more professional if we meet at one of our offices."

"You've seen mine. How about you show me yours?"

"Um—"

"Office, Holly. Show me your office."

"Of course," she said, sounding flustered. "I knew what you meant."

Okay, so he was teasing her on purpose now. Dammit, it felt good. Testing the waters, owning the moment, being assertive—weren't those all things a good CEO did naturally? It might not feel natural to him yet in the boardroom, but when it came to flirting with Holly, he was starting to get the hang of it.

He heard a tapping sound, and pictured her drumming a pen on her desk in a nervous rhythm. "Let's do my place. The office will be deserted after four thirty, since we're bussing the whole staff out to a big resort for the dinner. Might be the first time in history no one at First Impressions is working late."

"Except for you."

"Except for me."

"Well, Holly, I'm glad to be your exception. See you this evening."

Ben hung up, wishing like hell he could be her exception

in every way possible.

•••

Holly spent the last two hours of her workday fluctuating between two extremes. On one hand, she felt panicky about nailing this job with Ben and paying off the bank. She was used to handling pressure in her career, but unaccustomed to having a ticking clock dangling over her head, a perpetual reminder of what she stood to lose if she didn't succeed in her rebranding efforts with Ben.

On the other hand, she couldn't stop thinking about Ben. Not just about what his business could mean for the financial future of her company, but about his hands and lips and a lot of other body parts she couldn't stop picturing in her mind.

So when he walked through the door at four thirty-five wearing one of his new shirts and a well-cut pair of trousers, it was annoying to find herself staring slack-jawed at the man whose thumb prints were still on her thighs.

She closed her mouth and took a step forward, extending her hand. "Ben—so good to see you again. Welcome to First Impressions Public Relations and Branding."

He gave her an odd look, but he took her hand anyway. He shook it a few times but didn't let go as he surveyed the lobby and reception area. "Wow, this place is beautiful. Very hip. I love the galvanized steel wall."

"Thank you." Holly glanced down at their linked fingers and wondered if he realized he hadn't broken the handshake yet. She sure as hell wasn't going to be the one to tell him. "I chose all the slate myself, and the furniture is all mid-century modern stuff I found in flea markets and retro consignment shops."

"I love those chairs."

"Thanks. The couch is my favorite. It looks like something

you'd see on *Mad Men*, doesn't it?" She gestured toward the orange leather sofa with her free hand, part of her hoping Ben didn't let go of her other one anytime soon. "There's another one that's similar in the conference room. Would you like a tour before we get started?"

"I'd love one. This is great getting to see where you work. How long have you been in PR?"

"Most of my career. I got my degree in marketing, but I was always drawn to the branding and public relations aspect of it."

"How come?"

"There's something inspiring about being a cheerleader for a product or service I really believe in. About making sure other people have the opportunity to see it the way I do, and recognize its true potential."

He grinned. "I like the idea that I'm now one of your products or services."

"It is a little weird for me," she admitted, though the weird part wasn't the job itself. It was the fact that being around Ben now made her feel like a middle school girl with her first crush.

God, this was inconvenient.

"Did you say you started the company?" he asked.

"Yes. With my friend, Miriam."

"Did you have a lot of investors?"

"No." Holly bit her lip, kicking herself for not having investors or for not figuring out a way to shoulder the business mortgage all by herself. Or maybe she could have just leased a piece of property—

"Miriam's my business partner," she said, forcing her mind back to the conversation at hand. "She's also a brilliant branding specialist. She started out as a graphic designer and she's got a great eye for color and design."

"I'd love to meet her sometime."

"She's the one I consulted before we went shopping with you the other night. In a roundabout way, she's responsible for dressing you."

"Only fair, since you're responsible for undressing me." He grimaced. "I meant the zipper. Helping me fix the zipper—"

"It's okay, I knew what you meant." Holly felt the heat creeping into her cheeks, so she turned toward the lobby to continue the tour. "We offer a wide range of marketing services at First Impressions, but branding and rebranding is our specialty."

"Are these all awards you've won?"

She nodded toward the plaques and certificates on the wall, feeling a swell of pride in her belly. "We have a very talented team here."

"I can see that."

Something about his interest in her career left her wondering whether Chase had ever shown this much curiosity about her job. At one point not long after their honeymoon, he'd stopped by her office to take her to lunch and spent an hour visiting with her employees. At first, Holly had been thrilled with the attention, delighted by his interest in her career and his effort to get to know the people who made up her circle of friends and professional acquaintances.

It wasn't until later she'd realized he'd been snooping around for ammunition, eager to prove to Holly that she needed to cut back her hours.

"Marla in payroll said you've been very supportive of her choice to work part-time after having a baby," Chase had said later, twining his fingers through her hair to loosen her chignon.

"Her name is Mara," Holly had replied slowly, wondering why he'd taken an interest. "But yes, I helped her work out a job-share arrangement with another payroll specialist who also wanted to work part-time. It's gone well so far."

"Hmm," Chase had murmured. "So hypothetically speaking, you're in support of a woman putting her family first before her career."

"Of course," Holly said a little too quickly. "Or finding a way to balance the two—it's up to the individual woman, of course." She remembered the sinking feeling in her gut, the knowledge of what was coming next.

"So you're saying family isn't important to you *personally*?" Chase had challenged.

"Wow, are these ad concepts something you guys came up with?"

Ben's deep voice jarred Holly from the unpleasant trip down memory lane. She blinked, then followed his gaze to the magnetic board covered with a colorful array of ad slicks. He pointed to one, and she nodded, pleased to see he'd zeroed in on the concept she'd personally developed.

"Yes, that's for a new advertising campaign we've been working on for a kombucha brewer that's suddenly getting national media attention. These were mock-ups for a print campaign we showed them this morning."

"Did they like it?"

"Very much. The whole team invested a lot into the pitch, and the company owners could tell."

"Which one's yours?"

Holly shrugged. "Everything is a team effort around here. No one person gets credit for a concept or a pitch."

Ben grinned and shoved his hands in his pockets. "Sure, but just between you and me, I'm betting one of these has a little more of you in it."

She hesitated, then leaned past him to point at one of the ad slicks, conscious of the heat radiating from his body. "That one right there. The one with the dog and the grapes."

"I thought so. Very clever. It looks like something you'd

come up with."

She smiled, pretty sure it was the first time someone she'd known less than a week had been able to pick her work out of a lineup. "Thank you." She cleared her throat. "Shall we get started on the speech coaching?"

He turned to face her, his expression somewhere between resignation and amusement. "You mean you didn't invite me here to ogle your—work?"

"You're welcome to ogle my—*work*—all you want. But our time might be better spent if you do it while I'm offering you tips on public speaking."

"All right then. Shall we do it right here?"

"Let's move to the conference room." She led the way, conscious of Ben falling into step behind her. She'd worn her hair up in a chignon, and the exposed nape of her neck tingled with the thought of his breath on her bare skin.

She rounded the corner and halted just inside the conference room, then turned to Ben and gestured for him to join her. "I imagine this might be a similar space to the one where you'll be presenting?"

He stepped past her and nodded as he surveyed the room. "Langley Enterprises doesn't have a cool purple conference room table, but yes—the setup is probably pretty similar. Whiteboard, giant presentation screen, a big, ominous table with way too many chairs for way too many people."

"Haven't you heard that old public speaking tip about picturing your audience in their underwear?"

"Since my dad will be there, I'd rather not."

Holly laughed and moved to the front of the room. "After we get started, I'm going to have you do some visualization stuff where you imagine bodies in each of those chairs."

"As in cadavers or Victoria's swimsuit models?"

"Whatever rolls your socks up."

Ben sighed and pulled out a chair and slumped down into

it, folding his hands on the table. Holly tried not to stare at them. God, they were huge.

"So where do we start?" he asked. "Guide me, Obi-Wan Kenobi."

"*Star Trek* again?"

He widened his eyes, then pantomimed stabbing himself through the chest. "Are you kidding me?"

"What?"

"*Star Wars.* Holly, Obi-Wan Kenobi is from *Star Wars.* How can you confuse the two?"

"For starters, I've never seen either one. I only got your *Star Trek* reference the other night because I had a roommate who was really into it."

Ben shook his head in mock dismay. "How is it possible we're from the same planet?"

"I've been wondering the same thing myself."

He grinned and leaned further back into the chair, stretching his legs out in front of him. "One of these days, we'll have to have a *Star Wars* marathon."

Holly bit her lip, not sure whether the idea thrilled her or just created more potential for temptation. She was saved from deciding when he swung the subject back to the task at hand.

"Sorry, I didn't mean to digress from the purpose of our meeting. Where were we?"

"You asked me for public speaking tips," Holly reminded him. "Here's one: get your butt out of the chair."

He grinned and straightened up in his seat, but didn't stand. "You mean I can't deliver a sales presentation from a seated position?"

"You order drive-thru tacos from a seated position. You watch bad sci-fi from a seated position. You use the bathroom in a seated position."

"Hey, I'm a guy—"

"My point is that you need to establish a commanding presence right off the bat." She moved across the front of the room, keeping her posture straight in illustration. "You have your height, Ben. Use it to your advantage. Take charge of the room right from the start."

Looking bemused, he stood up. Holly stared up at him, startled by the sheer size of him again.

"Better?" he asked.

"Much." She took a step back, needing to put a little space between them. "Okay, that's a starting point. So tell me about this sales presentation. What are you going to be discussing?"

"Substrate-level phosphorylation in the absence of a respiratory electron transport chain."

She stared at him. "Was that in English?"

Ben shoved his glasses up on his nose. "I might have to dial it back a little for the intended audience."

"Unless your intended audience is comprised of nuclear physicists, I'd say that's an accurate assessment."

"The audience is a team of executives from Kleinberger. Some of the same guys you met the other night."

"Aren't they a brewing company?"

"Yep. Second largest craft brewery in the nation, and we're trying to sell them some top-of-the-line fermentation equipment we've engineered and manufactured. It's going to revolutionize their whole process."

"So—beer? You'll be talking about beer?"

"In a roundabout way, I guess so."

"Well, there's a topic you know and love. Why don't you start there?"

"Maybe. But I also need to discuss the engineering aspect of things."

Ben shoved his hands in his pockets, but Holly shook her head. "Nope, no slouching, no sitting, no hands in pockets. You're in a boardroom, not a video arcade."

"That's unfortunate. I'd be a lot more excited about this if I got to play Frogger with the audience." His face brightened suddenly, and Holly thought for the hundredth time how attractive he was when he smiled for real. Then he pulled his hands out of his pockets and held up a jump drive. "I almost forgot, I have a PowerPoint presentation."

"Perfect! Let's take a look at it." She held out her hand, and he dropped the little device into her palm. It was warm from his body heat, and she had the ridiculous urge to press the little electronic gadget to her cheek just to feel something he'd kept snugged up against his thigh.

She ordered herself to stop thinking about Ben's crotch and start thinking about his presentation. "When did you put this PowerPoint together?"

"About an hour after my dad came into my office and asked me to do this. It's probably a little rough."

Holly dropped into a chair at the conference table and shoved the jump drive into the slot on the boardroom laptop. She waited as the computer brought up a list of files. There was only one to display. "Is this it? Kleinberger Sales Presentation."

"Yep, that's the one."

She clicked the file, then waited as the computer whirred and flashed. When the PowerPoint file popped up, Holly stared at it for a few beats. "Your presentation is titled Eukaryotes, Glucose, and You."

"Too long?"

"Too—well, a lot of things." She clicked through a few of the slides, dismayed to see they all looked a lot like the first one. There were no graphics. Just a whole lot of really big words.

"Look, I have a great graphic designer who does amazing PowerPoint work," she said. "Let me give this to her in the morning and see if she can spiff it up a little for you."

"I appreciate it." Ben shoved his hands in his pockets again, then grimaced and pulled them out. "Sorry. Okay, what's next?"

"Have you rehearsed any of what you want to say?"

"I have a few ideas. I could use help organizing them. What's the best way to approach that?"

"A good strategy is to present your information in an inverted pyramid." Holly folded her hands on the table in front of her, feeling more in control of herself now that they were talking about a subject she knew well. "In other words, you want to give your audience the flashiest, most pertinent, most important information right up front."

Ben quirked an eyebrow at her. "I'm talking about the metabolic process of converting sugar into alcohol. What part of that is flashy?"

"The part where it becomes beer."

"Good point."

"Let's try this a different way," she said, minimizing his PowerPoint slides on the screen. "Is there any cost savings involved? Projected outcomes? Anything that might make an audience of business professionals sit up and pay attention?"

"Good, that's good." Ben pulled a piece of scratch paper out of the basket at the center of the table and plucked a pen from behind his ear. He dropped into a chair beside Holly and began scrawling notes. "I have a couple ideas about that."

She watched his gaze move back and forth across the page as he scribbled furiously. The beautiful amber-flecked eyes flashed with excitement, and his massive hand made the pen look like a toy. Whatever he was jotting, he seemed enthusiastic about it.

Why was that so sexy?

"Do you anticipate any really tough questions from the audience?" she prompted, crossing her legs to keep her mind off the thought of having Ben between them. "Any flaws in your plan that they might be inclined to zero in on?"

Ben glanced up and gave her a thoughtful look. "Well, I guess they might ask how Langley Enterprises' equipment differs from that of our closest competitors."

"And how *does* your equipment differ?"

"My equipment is huge. Much bigger than anyone else's equipment."

Holly gripped the edge of the table. "What?"

"The fermentation tanks," he said, giving her a funny smile. "They're quite large. I developed them myself, and they're capable of brewing up to five hundred barrels of beer in a twenty-four-hour period. That's pretty huge."

"It sounds like it," Holly said faintly. "What else?"

"Mine's also much harder."

"Oh. Well—"

"The metal Langley used, I mean. It's a 440C stainless steel I developed with a specific formulation of chromium and nickel designed for strength and corrosion resistance."

"Good," she said, nodding to reassure herself there was nothing sexual about this conversation. Nothing at all. "And you say you developed it yourself?"

"Yes, I was the head engineer on the project." He beamed proudly, leaning forward and spreading his hands wide.

Don't look at his hands, don't look at his hands, don't look—

"I made some very exciting developments with minerals," Ben said. "No one's ever utilized this exact formulation of materials to create equipment used in the brewing process before, so it's extremely revolutionary. I melded the stainless steel with a unique mineral blend of fukalite—"

"I'm sorry, what?"

"Fukalite. It's a calcium carbonate silicate hydrate mineral."

"Fukalite." She stared at him. "Did you just make that

up?"

He grinned. "Google it. F-U-K-A-L-I-T-E."

She looked at him for a few beats, then down at the laptop. Moving her fingers over the keyboard, she typed in the letters and waited. "I'll be damned."

"I told you."

Holly looked up to see him smirking, and she wondered if it was the thrill of being right, or the thrill of being able to say something so innocently filthy to her. Or filthily innocent. Was filthily even a word?

God, she was losing it.

But it was clear Ben was gaining confidence here. Whatever the cause of it, it was exactly the demeanor she hoped to refine in him. Holly drew her hands off the laptop and wiped her palms on her skirt. "This is good stuff, Ben. Important information to share with your audience. It's also clear you're passionate about the subject, which is a key thing to get across in your presentation."

"Thanks. We reviewed a lot of this in the all-hands meeting last week."

"Excellent," she said, trying not to let her gaze drop to his hands. "Okay, what else? Tell me some more things you think your potential client will get excited about."

"Well, there's the elongation."

Holly swallowed hard. "Elongation?"

"Absolutely." Ben nodded to himself as he bent to scribble more notes, really getting into it now. "Greater elongation means the material is less prone to fracture. While that typically results in lower stiffness, that's not the case with the materials I've developed."

"Oh." Holly uncrossed and recrossed her legs. "So stiffness isn't a problem?"

Ben grinned again. "Not in this case."

"Good." She nodded, trying to keep her expression as

professional as possible. "You want to address that right up front with your presentation. Let them know you've thought of it already, then show them the logic and evidence that proves—um—whatever you said about size and stiffness and hardness."

Ben grinned wider and stood up, his long legs carrying him to the whiteboard in two easy strides. There was a certain spring in his step that told her he was feeling pumped up about the subject. That he knew it well, and felt confident about his approach.

God, why was that so damn sexy?

"This is really helping, Holly," he said as he picked up a dry erase marker. "Thanks for getting my gears turning here."

"Don't mention it." She cleared her throat again, wondering who turned up the heater in the conference room. "Um, okay, so tell me more about the elongation. You think this is something your audience will be concerned with?"

"Definitely. As I was saying, greater elongation often goes hand in hand with lower stiffness." He turned to the whiteboard and began scrawling a complicated-looking formula while Holly fought once more not to stare at his hands.

"And your equipment has the right amount of elongation?"

"It's perfect. See, elongation is usually expressed as a percentage of the length change over the initial measured length."

"Right. I'll see if the designers can work some details about elongation, stiffness, and length into the PowerPoint presentation." She took a deep breath, willing herself to stay focused, but it was so hard.

So hard. So damn hard.

"Okay, it's also important in any public presentation to have a very clear call-to-action," she said.

"Action?"

"Yes. What is it you're hoping your audience will do?"

Ben studied her for a moment, his amber-flecked gaze holding hers for a few beats longer than Holly expected. "Give it to me," he said. "Their business, I mean. I want them to give me their business."

She licked her lips. He had to know what he was doing, right? She honestly couldn't tell. Maybe it was all in her head, or under her skirt, to be more precise.

Then again, maybe he knew damn well he was turning her on. Did it matter, as long as he was embracing his inner alpha male?

Holly took a shaky breath. "Then tell them to give it to you. Clearly. And make sure you show them why that's a smart business decision."

He nodded and set the dry erase marker back on the shelf beside the whiteboard. "I'm thinking I'd like to go a little off-the-cuff with the actual presentation. Maybe have some notes to work from, but not have a rehearsed speech."

"Sounds like a good approach." Holly folded her hands on the table again, pretty sure she had her libido under control now. "Tell you what. Why don't you just pretend I'm in the audience and that you're giving your talk to me? I'll take a few notes and give you some pointers afterward."

Ben looked down at her, then nodded. "In the interest of full disclosure, I feel like I should tell you that from this angle, I can see straight down the front of your shirt."

"What?"

He nodded. "It's true. And it's unbelievably sexy. I'm pretty sure there's no blood left in my brain and it's very hard to concentrate."

Holly touched a hand to the front of her blouse and tried to feel indignant, but she couldn't muster it up. All this time, she'd been egging him on to speak his mind, to show confidence and ambition and to go after what he wanted.

Was it really so terrible if *she* was what he wanted?

"You're going to have plenty of distractions in the boardroom on Friday," she told him. "You need to learn to work with that and keep delivering your speech anyway."

He nodded thoughtfully, his knee brushing hers as he eased himself to sit on the edge of the table next to her. He was so close, she could feel the heat radiating through his pant leg. "Working with distractions is going to be tough for me."

"Why do you say that?"

"ADD. Makes it hard to stay on task."

"Really?"

"Yep. So I need to practice speaking with distractions. Seeing down the front of your shirt is actually quite helpful."

Holly laughed, as charmed by this confident iteration of Ben as she was aroused by him. "You want me to wave pom-poms around and juggle watermelons so you really get used to speaking with distractions?"

"Nope." Ben grinned again, his amber-flecked eyes flashing behind his glasses. "But I do have another idea."

"What's that?"

"I think you should take your clothes off."

Chapter Nine

The second the words left his lips, Ben wished he could take them back. Hadn't he promised himself he wouldn't be a skirt-chasing jerk like his dad?

And hadn't Holly made it damn clear she wanted to keep a professional distance between them? That there was no room in their working relationship for anything of a sexual nature?

And Ben wanted to respect that. He really, really did.

But he could have sworn he'd been feeling some sort of crazy sexual tension crackling in the air between them for the last twenty minutes. It made him bold, or maybe it was just the fact that he was getting to talk about a subject he knew well.

Whatever the case, the look on Holly's face told him she wasn't hating it.

"Take my clothes off," she repeated. "You want me to take my clothes off."

"Yes."

"You know, that's not a bad idea."

Ben blinked. "It's not?"

She reached for the top button on her blouse, fiddling with it as she spoke, and Ben felt his mouth start to water.

"I don't know if you noticed this, but you started off at the very beginning of this session with a very dry, no-nonsense tone," she said. "Your posture was atrocious, your eye contact terrible, your enunciation lousy, the pacing of your words—"

"I think I got it," he said. "I suck. Point taken."

"That's just it, though. The second you stood up and started talking stiffness and elongation and—"

"And looking down the front of your blouse?"

"Exactly! The instant all that happened, everything changed. You stood up straighter, you began speaking more clearly—hell, even your eye contact was better." She grinned. "When you weren't looking at my tits, anyway."

"That's true, I suppose." He slid off the edge of the table, relieved she wasn't offended. "I also liked watching you squirm when I talked about fukalite and the size of my equipment."

"Making me squirm makes you a better public speaker?" Holly slapped her hand on the table. "That's what it is!"

"That's what *what* is?"

"Power. Confidence. Control. That's what revs your engine. That's what brings out your authoritative inner-CEO."

"Not a bad theory," Ben said, wishing she'd move a little to the side so he could look down her shirt again. "So you're volunteering your body for the sake of my public speaking skills?"

"I suppose I might be."

Ben nodded and folded his hands in front of him. "I approve this plan."

"I'm not saying that, exactly, but you did give me an idea."

"Any idea that involves you taking off your clothes is a good one."

Holly rolled her eyes. "You know how I mentioned that

old trick about picturing your audience in their underwear?"

"Particularly awkward with that grade school chess tournament speech I mentioned."

"I think we should give it a shot."

"Give what a shot?" He was still hung up on the idea of seeing Holly naked so maybe he'd missed some of the specifics of the plan.

"Start your presentation. Focus on the things we've been talking about, from the order of your presentation to your body language while you're delivering it. Really pay attention to what you're doing."

"And not to your breasts."

"You said you wanted to learn to handle yourself better with public speaking distractions."

"I think handling myself will be the least of my issues if you're taking your clothes off." Ben cleared his throat. "Okay, so you'll remove an article of clothing for each section of the speech I get right?"

"More or less."

"Who makes the rules?"

"I do. My company, my rules."

He grinned. "You know, it goes both ways. I find it pretty hot when you're in take-charge career mode, too."

Something flashed in Holly's eyes, and Ben wondered if he'd struck a nerve somehow. She was looking at him like she wanted to take *his* clothes off, so something must be working here.

"Okay then," Holly said, fingering her top button with agonizing slowness. "Let's begin. Address me just like you plan to address your audience on Friday. Here, let's start with a little encouragement."

She flicked open the top button on her blouse. Ben tried not to stare, but then remembered staring might actually be the point. Well, part of the point, anyway.

What was the point again?

He looked away from Holly's cleavage. He felt dizzy, but he also felt in control. Confident. In command.

"Hello, ladies and gentlemen," he began. "Thanks for joining me here today to learn a little more about what Langley Enterprises can do for you. I'm really excited to share some of the new features of our newly-engineered Brewmaster 5000 deluxe fermentation system and how it can make Kleinberger Brewing even more amazing than it already is."

"Good," she said, undoing another button. "Sincere flattery and genuine passion. You're not just *saying* you're excited, you *sound* excited."

"I am," Ben said, meaning it in more ways than one. He strode across the front of the room and turned to the whiteboard. He picked up the dry erase marker and began to scrawl a few words on the whiteboard. "Is anyone here familiar with the term 'viscous fingering?'"

"Um—"

He turned from the whiteboard to see her looking flushed and beautiful as she stared at his hands. She uncrossed and re-crossed her legs again, and he wondered what she was thinking. "Viscous fingering is the formation of patterns in a morphologically unstable interface between two fluids in a porous medium, and I'd like to tell you how viscous fingering can help Kleinberger up its game in terms of the brewing process."

"Is this supposed to be turning me on?"

Ben grinned. "In the rectangular configuration, the system evolves until a single finger forms. In the radial configuration, the pattern forms fingers by successive tip-splitting."

Holly licked her lips. "I have no idea what you just said, but it sounded really good."

"Undo another button," he commanded, feeling bolder as he recapped the dry erase marker.

He watched as a smile played over Holly's lips, her lavender-gray eyes flashing with interest. She flicked open another button. Ben stared right into her eyes, not letting his gaze dip into the visible valley of cleavage. There'd be plenty of time for that.

"Another thing that sets the Langley Enterprises system apart is stimulated emission."

"God, yes."

"This process occurs when a photon interacts with an atom's electron, causing it to drop to a lower energy level. Now, before I explain how that applies to the brewing process, I'd like you to go ahead and undo another button."

She grinned. "My pleasure." She flicked open one button and another, then pulled the shirt open wide, shrugging it off her shoulders. She wore a lacy black bra and a salacious expression that made Ben's pulse kick up three notches. "I'm throwing in another button for your commanding presence in the boardroom."

"Glad to hear it," he said, wishing he had the same amount of control over the hard-on now straining against the front of his pants. Damn flat-front trousers didn't have a lot of extra room. He saw her gaze drop to his fly and knew she could see how much she was getting to him. How much she turned him on.

"As I was saying," Ben said, not entirely sure what he'd been talking about. There really wasn't much blood left in his brain. "If you turn to page six in your handouts, you'll see a detailed diagram of the new Brewmaster system. You'll notice from the screw positions that—"

"Screw positions, yes."

"—that the Langley engineering team thought of everything, right down to the hardware. Stripping won't be an issue…" He grinned at Holly. "Panties, please?"

He didn't expect her to reach up her skirt, and he really

didn't expect her to pull out a lacy black thong. She tossed it at him, making it the first time in his whole life he'd been pelted with underwear for talking about science.

God, it's good to be a geek.

Ben caught the panties and kept going. "The manufacturing process for this equipment is also quite unique to Langley Enterprises. Using a heated rod, we penetrate the backside of—"

"God," Holly said and tugged the fastener out of her hair, letting it fall free from her tightly wound bun. Her hair slid dark and liquid around her bare shoulders, and Ben felt pretty sure he wouldn't be able to focus much longer.

"You should definitely talk more about penetration and rods," she said. "Do those use fukalite to make them harder?"

"No. They're already hard enough."

"I can see that." She twisted a strand of hair around her finger. "Nice job improving your posture. No more slouching. You're very erect now."

"Thanks to you. I appreciate your pointers." He stared at her nipples, which were jutting sharply through the lace of her bra. Was she as turned on as he was, or just cold?

No way she's cold. It's a million fucking degrees in here with the air conditioner blasting.

Ben cleared his throat. "Let's turn our attention from the equipment for a moment and talk a bit more about Langley Enterprises. As you know, we're the number one engineering and manufacturing firm in the nation. We have distribution channels in forty-seven countries, and an annual budget of more than a billion dollars. Those are tools we have at our disposal to help clients like Kleinberger."

"Excellent," Holly said, nodding as Ben strode from the whiteboard to stand in front of her. "Money. Power. Prestige."

"Take off your bra."

"My pleasure."

She started to reach behind her for the clasp, elbows bent at an awkward angle. Her breasts pushed toward him, and Ben ached to reach out and touch them.

Screw it. She could say no if she wanted to, but—

"Yes," she gasped as Ben dropped to his knees on the floor in front of her and buried his mouth in her cleavage. The bra fell away, exposing her breasts to his lips, his tongue, his teeth. He used all of them at once, touching and tasting and savoring the feel of her against his lips.

If this is what being an assertive, take-charge CEO got him, he was ready to commit to the job for life.

He slid his palm down the side of her body, all the way down her thighs. When he reached the hem of her skirt, he pushed upward, baring one inch of flesh at a time. Her thighs were silky and bare, and she let them fall apart as Ben shoved the skirt up over her hips.

"Beautiful," he murmured, grateful he'd had the foresight to get her panties off. He leaned down and planted a kiss between her legs, slipping his tongue inside her. She was wet and hot and he was dying to taste her again.

"Stop," she said.

Ben stopped, raising his head as he dropped his hands to his sides. "Okay." He cleared his throat. "I'm sorry."

"No, I don't mean *stop*, stop—I just mean…" She licked her lips, then shot a pointed look at his crotch. "It's my turn."

"What?"

"You've already had your mouth on me. I want to have my mouth on you."

He opened his mouth to say something clever and witty, but all that came out was "Ungh."

But that didn't seem to deter her, and she slid out of her chair to kneel in front of him. Ben was still too dumbstruck to say anything, so he pressed his lips to hers and kissed her hard and deep. She slid her hands up his back, anchoring them on each of his shoulders as she drew her body tight against him. When he broke the kiss, she was breathing heavy.

"Stand up," she ordered. "I want to suck you."

Jesus Christ. Was there any phrase in the entire English language with more power to bring a grown man to his knees?

But that wasn't the position she needed him in, so Ben got to his feet, a little shaky and not entirely certain he should be doing this. "Are you sure—"

"Yes," she said. "I know what I said earlier, and I know I might regret this later, but honest to God, if I don't have you in my mouth in the next thirty seconds, I'm going to scream."

"Not the way I want to make you scream," he said, then groaned as she grabbed hold of his belt and began to unfasten it. Her hands were deft and sure, not fumbling at all with the buckle the way he might have done if he'd tried to perform any tasks requiring dexterity. It was all he could do to keep himself upright as she pulled down his zipper, then hooked her fingers under the elastic of his boxer briefs.

She tugged them down, and Ben felt his cock spring free, hard and throbbing and mere inches from her face. He started to make some inane wisecrack, but then her lips closed around him and he forgot how to form words.

"God, Holly," he growled as she drew him into her mouth. Her lips were warm and soft, and her tongue felt like it was everywhere at once. She sucked him deeper, the gentle suction leaving Ben dizzy. She swirled her tongue around him, taking her time, keeping the pressure constant as she drew back again.

She reached up and slid her hand around the base of his cock, making it an extension of her mouth as she pulled him in again, sucking harder this time. He watched her ease back, sliding him all the way out of her mouth.

She looked up at him, her eyes sparking with heat. "I guess I shouldn't be surprised you've got the dick to match the hands," she said, grinning as she took him into her mouth again.

Ben gave a strangled gasp and slid his fingers into her hair. He was gripping the conference table with the other hand, pretty sure he'd fall down if he didn't have something to hang on to. Holly sucked him in again, the pressure intensifying both in her mouth and in his brain. She felt so good, her mouth warm and wet and inviting, her tongue gliding over him like heated velvet.

He was getting dizzier now as her fingers tightened around the base of his shaft and she began to move faster, quickening her pace. The suction was so intense, Ben nearly passed out, and he could feel her tongue flicking over the head of his cock.

"Holly," he choked out. "I'm close. You should stop if you don't want—"

"Yes," she said as she sucked him deeper, squeezing his shaft with her fingers. Her eyes were closed, lashes resting soft against her cheeks as her dark hair fell over her shoulders.

Ben felt the first spasm grip him and he groaned, hoping like hell they were the only ones in the building. Her eyes flew open, those pale orbs locking with his as the pleasure knocked him back on his heels. His fingers tangled in her hair as the next wave hit him, then another and another and another until he was mindless and spent and so full of pleasure he couldn't see straight. He let his eyes close as Holly slowed to a gentle rhythm.

When he finally opened his eyes, she was grinning up at him. "Well," she said, wiping the back of her hand against the corner of her mouth. "I'd say you aced your first round of public speaking class. Well done."

"Jesus Christ." Ben shook his head, then unwound his fingers from her hair and held out his palm. She placed her hand in his, and he lifted her to her feet so he could cradle her against his body. "That was fucking amazing."

"Tsk-tsk," she said, squeezing him tight as she breathed against the front of his shirt. "No cursing in a presentation. The audience will find you crass and unimaginative."

"Fuck the audience."

Holly grinned. "You kinda just did."

...

Lucky for Ben, the real audience was every bit as receptive as Holly had been, though perhaps not in quite the same way.

"Great job, Ben," said the Kleinberger CEO as he made his way out of the boardroom on Friday afternoon. "You really killed it in there."

"I loved the insight into all the engineering innovations you've got going here at Langley," the CFO added. "I was fascinated by the details of stimulated emissions."

"Thanks," Ben said, his brain flashing on an image of Holly writhing at the conference table. "We did a lot of hands-on work with that."

"Yeah," Ben's dad said, clapping him on the shoulder hard enough to knock him sideways if he hadn't been braced for it, but he was, and his dad's hand seemed to bounce off his shoulder. "Too bad you forgot to mention the fact that we can put a copper finish on that tank so it matches their other equipment."

"I didn't forget, Dad, I just chose not to use it. My presentation, my bullet points."

"Well I say you did an outstanding job." Kleinberger's VP of cost analysis smiled at him. "You'll have our decision soon."

The executive team filed out of the room one by one, chattering amongst themselves as they went. The instant the door closed behind the last three-piece suit, Lyle turned to Ben.

"That wasn't too bad, boy."

"Thanks," Ben said. It wasn't the most enthusiastic praise he'd ever received, though it might have been the best he'd gotten from his dad. How many chess trophies had been brought home, or academic scholarships had he won without his dad uttering a single word of approval?

"Won't do you much good when it's time to run the company," his dad had said so often that Ben stopped bringing home awards from the science fair.

Now, his father was staring at him with something that almost looked like approval. "You want to go grab a drink and celebrate?" Lyle asked.

Ben hesitated. He almost said no, but something about his father's expression told him this was one of those rare opportunities for father/son bonding that he shouldn't pass up. "Sure. Just let me shut down my office. Want to meet across the street at Bailey's in ten minutes?"

"I'll grab a booth at the back."

Ben nodded and hustled back to his office, pulling his phone out of his pocket as he went. He set it on his desk and went through the motions of shutting down his computer, grabbing his jacket, waiting impatiently for his phone to power on.

He hadn't talked to Holly all week, not since she'd walked him to the door after the mother of all speech coaching sessions.

"Thanks for coming by, Ben," she'd said as she hesitated at the front door of First Impressions, all business once they had their clothes back on. Her hair had even been tucked back up in its neat little bun, and Ben had ached to undo it again. "I hope the speech coaching was helpful."

"Helpful doesn't even begin to describe what just happened in there."

She'd smiled and blushed and looked down at her hands.

"I guess I got a little carried away."

"You can get carried away anytime with me."

She'd sighed and looked up at him again, her expression troubled. "Look, Ben—"

"I know, I know—you're going to tell me you don't normally do this and that it can't happen again?"

"Right. Something like that." She bit her lip. "I've just got a lot going on in my life right now. I really need to focus on my career and revenue and—well, business."

"Business," Ben repeated. "We're on the same page there. At the moment, I need to be eating, sleeping, and dreaming of nothing but business."

A dark light had flashed in Holly's eyes, but Ben wasn't sure what to make of it. He was still trying to think of something to say when she'd taken a step back from him.

"Let's just do our best to keep it professional, Ben. It feels like things are sorta even now, right?"

"Even?"

"You know. What happened at your place and then just now—"

"You make it sound like a business merger instead of the best damn blowjob of my life."

She'd laughed, giving him a playful swat as she stepped away. "Call me if you need any more public speaking tips between now and Friday. I'm sure you'll do great."

They were the last words she'd spoken to him, at least for now. He'd done his best not to call her, not even for a last-minute pep talk before the presentation.

But now that the presentation was over, surely it was okay to at least let her know? She was still his PR consultant, after all. There was no reason not to contact her.

He picked up his phone and typed out a quick text message.

Presentation went great. Thanks for all the tips! Couldn't have done it without you.

Then he shrugged into his jacket and jogged to the elevator, not wanting to keep his dad waiting.

By the time he sat down at the table, Lyle was already halfway through his glass of Laphroig. Ben slid into the booth across from him, not sure whether to be annoyed or grateful his dad had ordered one for him, too.

"Cheers, boy!" Lyle said as he held up his glass. "Let's hope the Kleinberger team makes the right decision."

"Cheers," Ben echoed, and picked up his own glass. He clinked it against his father's, then took a sip of the smoky brew. God, he'd probably never get used to it. For his father's sake, he wanted to like it, but he couldn't help but think he'd rather swill drain cleaner.

His phone buzzed in his pocket, and Ben put his hand on it.

Holly.

His stupid pulse started to gallop, but Ben left his phone where it was. He wasn't going to be that guy who checked messages while having a conversation with someone else. He owed his dad some undivided attention for at least the time it took to down a glass of Laphroig.

Ben looked down at his glass and scowled. It could be a while.

"Gotta love a good Irish whiskey," Lyle said. "This is the fifteen-year, of course."

Ben nodded and looked up at his dad. "Of course."

"Sure as hell wish they'd get the eighteen-year-old stuff here, or even the twenty-five, but at least it's not the ten."

"Thank God for small blessings."

He took another sip, relieved this one went down a little easier. He wondered if this was how normal fathers and sons interacted. Ben had no idea. His mom had died when he was at the age most boys were getting their driver's license. Instead, Ben had been heading off to college. He thought he'd been well past the age when he urgently needed a mother's snuggles or homemade cookies, but he'd craved those things anyway.

Lyle hadn't been up for any of that, save the stiff, one-armed hug he'd given at the funeral.

"Buck up, boy," Lyle had told him. "It's just you and me, now."

And it had been, for half of Ben's life.

Ben took another sip of whiskey and looked at his father across the table. "So do you think we'll get the Kleinberger deal?"

Lyle's eyes lit up the way they always did when anyone brought up business deals. "Yeah, I think we stand a good chance."

"And you think the presentation went well?"

Okay, fine, he was fishing. Was it so wrong to want approval from his father? Lyle leaned back against his seat and swirled the smoky liquid in his glass, staring down at it like it held the meaning of life. "It was good. 'Course, there's something missing."

"From the presentation? I covered all the bases. I thought the cost analysis was thorough without being overwhelming, and the—"

"No, not all that mumbo jumbo. I'm talking about you as the CEO."

"What about me?"

"Folks want to see a CEO with a little more charisma. A guy who can get out there and golf with the boys, then charm all the ladies at the company party."

Ben raised an eyebrow at his father and gripped his glass a little tighter. "Are you suggesting I hire professional escorts to pose as purveyors of my charms?"

"Oh, don't get all pissy. I'm talking your personal life. In the business world, folks like to follow the lead of a man all the women want. Now's the time for you to play the field a little, really show the ladies what you've got."

"I see," Ben said tightly. "And that's the secret to your success?"

"I have the advantage of being a widower. That's even better."

"Being widowed is a business asset?"

"Sure. It shows I'm grounded enough to get married and have a family in the first place, but not tied down by having to spend time with them."

Ben frowned down at his drink, more than a little annoyed to be lumped together with his dead mother as a professional advantage. Spending time with him or with Ben's mom had never been a priority for Lyle, not even when Judy was sick as a dog with the chemo.

Part of Ben still blamed his dad for all of that. For the sadness in his mom's eyes as she sat lonely and waiting for Lyle to come home from a business trip. For the science fairs Lyle never attended because he was off flirting with secretaries. For the missed chance at early diagnosis of the cancer that claimed Judy's life.

For all of it and then some.

But hell, at least his dad was trying to connect with him on some level now. Maybe that's what mattered. Maybe learning something from his father was his best shot at becoming the sort of CEO he needed to be to take the company to the next level.

Ben swirled the liquid in his glass, relieved to see there was a lot less of it now than there had been. "If we get the Kleinberger deal, the company would be well-positioned for a potential merger of—"

"How serious are you about that Honey girl?" Lyle asked, snapping his fingers. "The one you brought to the event."

"Holly?"

"Yeah, that's the one. Take her, for instance."

"Take her where?"

Lyle ignored him. "She's a pretty girl, but not someone you're planning to have a relationship with, right?"

Ben stared at his father, not sure if he was more annoyed by the old man's line of questioning, or by the fact that Holly had made it clear she had no interest in a relationship with him.

Why did that bother him so much?

Because you're starting to fall for her. Because you wouldn't mind a relationship one bit, but that's the last thing she wants.

"You've gotta play the field, boy," Lyle said. "That Hayley—"

"Holly."

"That Holly girl has to be getting up there in years. What is she, thirty?"

"I have no idea. And since when is thirty considered 'up there?'"

"Women have a clock, boy. They can't dick around for years building a career the way you and I can. They've gotta start squeezing out babies, making a home, all those things women want. And that's not what you want right now. You've gotta sow some oats."

Ben felt himself bristling at the notion that his father would have any idea what he wanted, much less what Holly wanted. *Especially* Holly. He opened his mouth to protest, but his dad was still talking.

"Holly's fine for now, but you've gotta think bigger picture."

"Bigger picture," Ben repeated, not entirely sure he and his father were speaking the same language.

"Now's not the time to be settling down. Now's the time for relationships that'll further your career in the long run."

Ben put his drink down. Is that what Holly was to him? A stepping stone in his career path?

He stood up, suddenly overcome by a need to talk with her, to prove to himself that's not how things were. That Holly could be more to him than a surface relationship crafted to get him ahead in the business world.

"Where are you going, boy?"

Ben was already out of his seat with his phone gripped in his hand. "I think I need to call someone."

"Is this someone who can get us ahead with the Kleinberger guys?"

"I suppose so."

His dad beamed his approval. "Then get to it."

Chapter Ten

"So let me get this straight," Miriam said, stretching her long legs out beside Holly's kitchen table and displaying an impressive pair of red leather Manolo Blahniks. "Ben went down on you at his place, then you sucked him off in our conference room, but you're totally not breaking your no-sex-with-a-client rule because he hasn't actually penetrated your vagina with his penis?"

Holly winced and gripped the stem of her wineglass a little tighter. "I know it sounds terrible—"

"No, it sounds like some sort of weird afterschool special." Miriam took a sip of her own wine, then reached out and put a hand over Holly's. "Honey, you think maybe you're trying a little too hard to stick to these weird, arbitrary rules you've invented?"

"I don't know. Hell, I don't know anything anymore." Holly shook her head and grabbed a potato chip out of the bowl at the center of the table. "I thought I found commanding and take-charge men a turnoff, and then I dropped to my knees in front of one."

"Not all take-charge guys are pigs, you know."

"I don't even know if Ben *is* a take-charge guy. Maybe I'm bringing out the worst in him."

"A guy who can get you off with his tongue or get you on your knees with his science vocabulary doesn't sound like the worst to me."

Holly sighed and took another sip of wine. "The thing is, I pegged him as more of a beta guy, which I kinda liked after being with an alpha guy for all those years. So why the hell am I turned on by the alpha version of him?"

"Old habits die hard?"

Holly shook her head. "I don't think so. He couldn't be more opposite of Chase if they were a different species."

"Thank God for that. Speaking of King Asshole, what's the latest from the bank?"

Holly sighed. "Not much. Obviously, I have to complete the job for Ben Langley before we're paid in full. The first check helped, but it's not the full amount I need to refinance the loan so it's solely in my name."

"And Chase isn't budging on his timeline?"

"I haven't been able to reach him. He's handling everything through his lawyers, just peppering me with legal documents about how I have until the end of next month to either sell or get his name off the loan."

"Does he know refinancing a loan when it's underwater is about as likely as the possibility he'll spontaneously combust?" Miriam's eyes lit up. "Hey, there's an idea."

"I don't think he cares." Holly bit her lip. "Miriam, I'm so sorry. I know it seemed like a good idea when we started out to buy the building. Real estate prices were so low, and having my husband co-sign the loan didn't seem like such a dumb move at the time. If I'd had any idea—"

"Don't," Miriam said. "You can't blame yourself. Hell, I wasn't in a position to get any sort of loan at all. My credit was in shambles back then or I would have helped. This isn't anyone's fault." She cocked her head to one side. "Well, it might be Chase's fault a little."

"God, I can't believe I married a guy who thought my career was his rival."

"I wouldn't have *let* you marry him if he'd acted like that at the start. It wasn't until he started climbing the corporate ladder at his firm that it all seemed to go to his head."

Holly nodded as her thoughts strayed to Ben. How would the CEO position change him? Polishing his social skills and confidence was one thing, but were there other things about him that might change?

"So back to Ben," Miriam said, reading her thoughts. "You said he's showing signs of being a more take-charge guy?"

"Yes." Holly pressed her lips together and tried to keep her thoughts professional instead of letting them stray to the other ways Ben could take charge. "I've been working with him on it, of course, but honestly, I think just being in a position of power is bringing it out in him."

"That's probably not the only position that's bringing out his inner alpha male." Miriam grinned. "Who knew hooking up with your client was exactly what you needed to bring out his inner beast?"

"Right," Holly said, grabbing another chip. "So whatever's been happening between us is just a technique to take his career to the next level. There's nothing more to it."

"You keep telling yourself that."

"Come on, Miriam. My job is to further this guy's career. I'm being paid well to do that right now, but there's sure as hell no future in a relationship with that dynamic. Been there, done that, *divorced* that. End of story."

"I don't think that's it, hon. Maybe there could be more if you wanted it."

"I don't want it," Holly insisted, pretty sure that was true. "I should probably stop falling into bed with the guy, though."

"Technically, you haven't fallen into bed with anyone. There's been a living room floor, a conference room floor—"

"I can't believe I keep falling onto the floor for this guy."

Miriam sipped her wine, considering. "That doesn't have the same ring to it."

Holly buried her head in her hands, knowing she should probably feel guiltier than she did. She'd get to the guilt in a minute, but right now she couldn't stop thinking about the feel of him in her mouth, the way he gripped her hair and groaned her name as he came.

"I have to stop this," she said. "With Chase and the bank breathing down my neck, it's completely stupid for me to go risking the most lucrative client I have right now."

"Are you sure Ben's not becoming more than a client?"

"What do you mean?"

"I see the look in your eye. You're smitten with the guy."

"I can't be."

"Whatever you say." Miriam gave her a knowing look, then picked up her wineglass and drained the last of it before glancing at her watch. "Look, sweetie, I have to get home and feed Phuzeei. Not that my cat is more important than your needs right now, but—"

"No, it's fine. I've been whining to you long enough."

"It's not whining. It's never whining when there are orgasms involved." Miriam stood up and Holly followed suit. "You'll be fine, hon. Besides, he's obviously happy with your professional services. Blowjobs aside, he likes what you're doing for him."

"I'm glad his presentation went well."

"And the rest of this rebrand will go well, too. As for the loan—" Miriam trailed off, looking a bit less confident. "Well, if worse comes to worst, we can run the business out of a cardboard box and brand the whole concept as the hot new minimalist trend."

"Ugh. I'm going to be fretting about it all weekend, you know. Like what if the money doesn't come through for some reason?"

"Try not to think about it. There's nothing else you can do right now anyway, and worrying will just make you sick." Miriam strode toward the door, Prada handbag looped over one arm as Holly followed behind her. "Are you in for the night?"

"I think so. I'm exhausted from all the stress about money. I'm just going to put on some pajamas and crawl into bed."

Miriam grinned. "Put on the cashmere ones he bought you. Besides being luxurious, they're probably dripping with his pheromones."

"There's a nice mental picture."

"Good night." Miriam bent down and gave her a hug. "Have a good weekend."

Holly hugged back, then closed the door behind Miriam, not feeling a whole lot better than she had when her friend had stopped by an hour ago after the event. Then again, she didn't feel worse.

She glanced at her phone, wondering if she'd hear from him again. After he'd texted to let her know the presentation had gone well, she'd texted back a brief message congratulating him. She hadn't heard from him since.

Holly trudged to the bedroom to put on her pajamas. Okay, fine—she put on the ones she'd gotten from Ben. Was that so wrong? They were comfortable, and they were new.

The shirt still smelled like his aftershave, and Holly resisted the urge to hold it up to her nose and breathe in his scent before pulling it over her head. Her whole body did a happy little swoon at the memory of what she'd been doing the last time she'd worn this top.

Outfitted in her comfy attire, she wandered into the kitchen, her mind still drifting to Ben's presentation. Had her speech coaching tips made a difference for him in the presentation? She hoped she'd managed to impart at least a few helpful hints before getting derailed by chemistry or lust or whatever the hell kept seizing control of her brain and making her do crazy things.

God, why was she taking so many risks lately? Langley Enterprises was a huge client—the biggest First Impressions had ever landed. Between Ben's rebranding work and the potential for more Langley business, this was her best shot at earning enough to refinance the loan. She was chancing a lot by fooling around with Ben. Jeopardizing her whole career for what?

For a man. You swore you'd never do that.

Holly sighed and yanked open her freezer door, determined to drown her sorrows in something sinfully sweet. She spotted a gallon of vanilla ice cream and thought about the ice cream floats Ben had made the other night.

"Bingo!" she said aloud as she pulled open the fridge to find a liter of strawberry seltzer Miriam had left behind. It wasn't root beer, but it would do.

She set about making herself a float, wondering what Ben was up to. Was he celebrating? The thought of a celebration that included scantily clad women throwing themselves at a powerful man was enough to deepen her glum mood, so she put an extra big scoop of ice cream in her float.

She'd just shoved the ice cream back in the freezer when her phone rang. She picked it up with the ice cream scoop still clutched in her other hand. "Hello?"

"Hey, Holly. It's Ben. Open your front door."

A shudder of excitement ran through her, followed by a shudder of dread. She probably looked like she was having a seizure, which was hardly the condition she wanted to be in for having company. Besides, she was wearing the loungewear he'd bought her. The last thing she needed was Ben thinking she'd been pining away for him in her pajamas.

Then she imagined him standing there on her front porch, and her brain started to cloud with the thrill of spending an evening with him. "You want to come in?"

Her body was already moving toward the front of the house in defiance of her brain's warning that it wasn't a good idea. She had the ice cream scoop clutched in one hand and a stupid grin on her face, which she spotted in the mirror on her way to the door.

"I'm not at the door but something else is," Ben said.

Holly stopped at the door, her hand on the knob. "Okay, this is starting to sound slightly creepy stalkery."

"I thought you liked creepy stalkery. At least you did when I bought you pajamas."

"That's true." She hesitated, her hand still on the door. "Apparently I'm turned on by creepy stalkers and dirty-talking science geeks. How did I never know this about myself until I hit thirty?"

"You're thirty?"

"Yes, why?"

"That's what my dad thought."

"Why was your dad guessing my age? Never mind, how old are you?"

"Thirty-one. Did you open your door yet?"

"Hang on." Holly set the ice cream scoop on the entry table and cracked open her front door. Sitting on the front stoop in the beam of her porch light was the biggest arrangement of wildflowers she'd ever seen.

"Ben, they're beautiful!" Cradling the phone against her ear, she bent down to scoop up the basket. "Oh my God, did you bring these?"

"I had them delivered."

"They're gorgeous." She carried the basket into the house, kicking the door shut behind her. "Thank you."

"No, thank *you*. Without your coaching, I never could have nailed that presentation today."

"I was just doing what you hired me to do."

"You did a little more than that."

Holly winced as she set the basket on the table, but before she could say anything about the fact that she didn't usually suck off clients in her boardroom, Ben beat her to it.

"No—uh, I didn't mean that. Well, *that* was nice, too, but it's not what I'm talking about. You really lit a fire under me."

"What?"

"The passion you were talking about making sure I infuse into my presentation. I nailed it."

She grinned and moved the phone to her other ear, turning the flower arrangement from one side to the other to see which way looked best. "I'm so happy for you."

"You should have seen me in there. I really took charge, really controlled the room and let my excitement take over."

"I wish I could have been there."

"Me, too. And I wish I could see you now."

Holly bit her lip, wishing she could invite him over. Would it be the worst thing? Maybe they could just—

"No." She startled herself by speaking aloud, but now that she'd said it, she knew it was the right thing. "I wish we could get together, Ben, but we both know how that would end up."

"I know. I'm on board with that. Totally in agreement with not seeing each other. That's why we're going to have a movie night together."

Holly clutched the phone tighter. "Did you miss the part where I said it would be a bad idea if we got together?"

"Nope, I heard you loud and clear. And I agree."

"You do?"

"Yep. Open the card attached to the flowers."

She hadn't noticed the card before, but now that she saw it, she realized it was a lot bulkier than a normal envelope. It was square and thick and looked like it held more than a card. "What's in there?"

"Open it."

She plucked the envelope out of the sea of daisies and sunflowers, tearing into it with embarrassing enthusiasm. She stared at the packaging for a moment, then laughed. "You bought me a *Star Wars* DVD?"

"It's the same one I have. The collectors' edition. So I figure if we both put it in at the same time—"

"We'd avoid the temptation to put something else in."

Ben laughed. "Pretty much. Are you game?"

"Definitely."

"Good. Go grab a snack and put your jammies on."

"Done and done."

"Yeah? What's your snack?"

"A strawberries and cream float. I just invented it."

"Sounds delicious. Okay, so I'll meet you in bed in thirty seconds."

Holly felt a jolt of excitement at his words and wondered what it would be like to have him mean it for real. Instead, she scooped up her dessert and the DVD and trudged toward the back of the house. "How'd you know I have a TV in my bedroom?"

"Lucky guess. If we're going to pretend-snuggle, it's better to do it in a bed than on the couch."

She laughed and set the froth-filled glass on her nightstand. "You want the right side or the left?"

"Right."

"Good. The left side is mine. Hang on a sec, let me put it in—"

"God, yes."

She laughed and rolled her eyes. "The DVD, you goof. If

this is going to turn into a phone sex session, I'm hanging up."

No you're not, her libido telegraphed.

Still, she felt a little relief when Ben didn't pursue that line of conversation. Not that she wouldn't love talking dirty with him. But there was something about the idea of a quiet evening of watching a movie together and snuggling that made her feel warm inside.

Okay, *virtual* snuggling. But even that sounded nice.

"Got it all cued up?" Ben asked.

"Hang on. I don't watch a lot of movies, so it'll take me a second to get it going."

She fumbled the DVD out of its case and maneuvered it into the machine, then picked up the remote control. She scampered back to bed and threw the covers back, then burrowed beneath a thick layer of blankets.

"What size bed do you have?" he asked.

"A queen. Why?"

"Just trying to picture it. How about your covers?"

"I have a down-filled comforter with a purple cover on it and this crazy-looking afghan hand-knitted with every color of yarn on the planet."

"You knit?"

"Nope. I always wished I could, but I don't have the patience. Maybe someday. My grandma made it."

"That's sweet," he said, his voice low and even. "May I fluff your pillow for you?"

"Why does that sound dirty when you say it?"

"Anything sounds dirty if you say it right."

"Example?"

"Mastication-induced arousal."

"What?"

"It's a term used to describe the beneficial cognitive effects of chewing," he said. "Or how about antennating?"

"Is that a cross between penetrating and lubricating?"

"Now who's talking dirty? It's just the term to describe how insects communicate by touching antennae."

"That sounds romantic."

"It kinda does, doesn't it?" She heard rustling on the other end of the line, and imagined Ben snuggling back into his own nest of blankets. Did he have a bed in his penthouse yet, or was he sleeping on the floor? She hadn't had a chance to find out the other night, and now didn't seem like the right time to ask.

"Okay, are you all settled in?"

"Yes," Holly said, nestling back against her own pile of pillows. "Ready."

"I'm going to count us down from three. When I say go, hit play."

"Got it. Are we watching the previews, or skipping them?"

"Which do you prefer?"

"Skip."

"Okay. Go ahead and cue it up."

Holly hit a couple buttons on her remote, then hit pause. "Ready," she said.

"Good. Okay then. *Three—*" His voice was low and sexy and left no doubt he'd be amazing at phone sex if he tried. "*Two—*"

"Wait. Are you wearing pajamas, too?"

"Nope."

"What are you wearing?"

"I thought we weren't having phone sex."

"We're not," she said, flushing a little as she picked up her glass. "I just want to be able to picture you. If we're virtual-snuggling, you've gotta set the scene."

"Fair enough. I'm wearing boxers."

"No shirt?"

"No shirt."

She ignored the pulse of pleasure that shot through her

as she picked up her ice cream float and took a sip. It was amazing. "What's your snack?" she asked.

"Root beer float and a bowl of popcorn."

"Just like the other night."

"Not quite."

The smile in his voice sent a fresh wave of excitement coursing through her body, but she scooped up another bite and closed her eyes. "Okay, I can picture you snuggled up in bed in your boxer shorts with your popcorn and your—"

"No bed. I haven't gotten around to getting one yet."

"What? Where are you sleeping?"

"A sofa. It's quite large and very comfortable. I just need to find time to get back to the furniture store to pick out the rest of the things I need."

The idea of Ben sleeping on a couch in his gazillion dollar penthouse gave her a tickle of guilt, and she almost opened her mouth to invite him to share her bed for real.

But she stopped herself. He was a big boy. He could get a hotel room with a bed if he needed one. Right now, she needed the security of knowing she could keep her distance. That she could keep her professional composure and still have a relationship with this guy.

"Okay, so you're snuggled up in a blanket nest on the sofa," she said. "And you've got your snack."

"Yep. Got your remote?"

"Yes." She took another sip of her float. "My feet are a little cold. Can I put them on you?"

Ben laughed. "Sure. Here, let me scoot over so you can snuggle under my arm and get warm. Better?"

"Much," she said, closing her eyes as she imagined herself leaning her head against Ben's chest. She sighed with pleasure, the glass chilly in her hands, her feet somehow toasty now, and somewhere in the middle—right around her heart—she felt absolutely perfect.

"Okay then," Ben said. "Three, two, one, *play*."

Holly opened her eyes and hit the button, then watched as the 1977 version of the Twentieth Century Fox logo flashed across the screen. The image faded, giving way to a sea of brightly colored words on a black screen.

"A long time ago in a galaxy far, far away—" Ben murmured.

She closed her eyes again, giving herself over to the steady hum of his voice, the softness of the blankets, the smooth richness of her dessert.

And the terrifying suspicion she was falling for Ben Langley.

...

The next morning, Ben was still warm all over from his night of make-believe snuggling with Holly. Unlike his teen years when his social awkwardness and rapid advancement through school had made imaginary girlfriends the only kind he could get, Holly was all real. Even virtual-cuddling with her felt better than real intimacy with most women had.

Of course, that didn't detract from the fact that touching her for real had been mind-blowing. Both times. He ached to have his mouth on her again, to feel her writhing beneath his palms and hear those soft gasps of pleasure as he touched and tasted and stroked her.

God, he was losing his mind.

He kept himself busy all morning, working on spreadsheets and sales reports and going over the figures for a new client they were bidding on. Anything to keep his mind off having Holly again.

When his phone rang at eleven and he saw her name on the readout, Ben's heart nearly surged out of his chest.

"Holly," he said, leaning back in his chair. "Is life vastly improved for you now that you aren't the only person on the planet never to have seen *Star Wars*?"

She laughed. "Yes. Losing my *Star Wars* virginity to you has been life-changing. I just finished doing my hair in Princess Leia braids."

"That's the hottest thing I've ever heard in my life."

"Now I almost feel guilty for disappointing you when you see me."

"I'm going to see you?" Ben winced at the giddy note in his own voice, but Holly didn't seem to notice.

"You are if you accept my proposal. I was thinking about the fact that you still don't have a bed—"

"This idea just keeps getting better."

"Down, boy. Remember when we first met at the furniture store and you were being eaten alive by that sales clerk?"

"Vaguely. Was that when I got kissed by some strange woman I'd never met?"

"*You* kissed *me*, Langley. Which was about the only assertive thing you did."

"Give me a break. I was jet-lagged."

"And now you're not. Plus you've been working on being in control and commanding. Wouldn't it be good practice for you to walk back into that furniture store and try out your new assertiveness in the same environment?"

Ben wasn't sure he loved the idea itself, but the thought of seeing Holly again was enough to convince him. "How about I pick you up in thirty minutes?"

"Really? You mean you're up for it?"

"Sure, why not? You're right, it'll be good practice. Are you going to require me to beat aggressive saleswomen over the head with lamps, or is it sufficient to politely refuse their advances?"

"I think I'm going to need you to stop short of actual violence."

"That's too bad. I was looking forward to kicking some ass."

Holly laughed. "Say that again a few times and maybe it'll sound less awkward coming out of your mouth."

"And this is where, as a gentleman, I politely refrain from twisting your words to remark upon the likelihood of coming *in* your mouth."

"Jesus Christ, Ben." Her voice sounded more shocked and breathy than offended, but he still wasn't sure if he should apologize until she spoke again.

"You've got a good head start on the assertive vocalization," she said. "Pick me up in thirty minutes and you can talk dirty to me all the way to the furniture store."

Chapter Eleven

Despite what Holly had said on the phone, Ben refrained from talking dirty to her in the car. It wasn't that he didn't want to. It was more that he wanted to prove to her this could be more than a surface fling. That he wasn't just another jerk like his dad whose only use for relationships was as rungs on his career ladder.

Okay, so that crack he'd made about coming in her mouth had been taking it too far, though she hadn't seemed to mind. Hell, if he read things right, it even turned her on.

But was he wrong for wanting more than that? For thinking they could be more than just a business-based dalliance?

Ben shushed his inner critic as he hit his turn signal and took the exit toward the furniture store. The vehicle was new, an embarrassingly flashy sports car his father had urged him to buy a few days ago. Ben had been perfectly happy with his old Volvo, but his dad insisted the CEO of a multi-billion dollar company shouldn't be driving a car that still had his college bumper stickers on the back.

"Get a real car, dammit," Lyle told him. "Something that'll make people sit up and take notice."

Ben had to admit, the car was pretty nice. Or maybe it was just the view of Holly in the passenger seat with her long legs bare against the leather seat and her dark hair rustling in the breeze from the air conditioner.

"Are those your golf clubs in back?" she asked.

"Yes. Why?"

"I thought you hated golf."

"I do."

She gave him an odd look. "So you're driving them out into the country to leave them for dead?"

"Nah, I'm trying to build a relationship with them. I figure if I carry them around for a while, maybe play some nice music and show them a bit of scenery, we'll warm up to each other."

"Sounds like a good dating strategy. If you're lucky, maybe they'll put out."

Ben laughed. "I've been playing a little bit after work lately. Just a few holes here and there, trying to get the hang of it. I'm actually pretty good."

"I'm not surprised. It's a good game to know for business. I had to learn a few years ago."

She sounded less than thrilled about that, and Ben wondered if there was a story behind it. "I'm playing Tuesday night if you want to join me," he offered.

"Thanks, but I've got a client meeting."

"I'll be on the Vandermeer Course," he said, hoping to tempt her. "Normally it takes months to get a tee time there, but I pulled a few strings. If you want to blow off your client meeting—"

"I don't," she said, and her sharp tone seemed to surprise them both. "I mean it's an important meeting. I make it a policy never to set aside my business interests for someone else's."

"Sorry," he said, annoyed with himself for ruffling her feathers. "I wasn't inviting you for business, though. Just for fun."

"Everything's about business," she said. "Isn't that why you're learning to play golf?"

"True." Ben glanced over to see her studying him. "What?" he asked as a trickle of self-consciousness dribbled through his veins.

"I never realized how much you look like your dad."

"You're the second person who's said that to me this week."

"Who was the first?"

"Parker," he admitted. "It was after I showered at the gym, and he pointed out that he'd never seen me comb my hair with anything besides my fingers. Then he grabbed the monogrammed brush my dad gave me and chucked it in the toilet."

Holly laughed. "I can't decide if that's really sweet or really weird."

"Maybe a little of both. Parker's not a big fan of my father, in case you hadn't guessed."

"Of your father, or of you becoming your father?"

"All of the above. I think he's annoyed I blew off another boxing workout to play golf a few days ago."

"Huh," she said, and Ben heard the dark note again in that single syllable.

"Boxing might be more fun, but golf's a game I have to master if I'm going to fit in as the CEO of a major corporation."

"I suppose so," she agreed. "Still, if you hate it, there are plenty of other hobbies you can take up in the name of being a well-rounded CEO."

"You mean like skirt chasing and day drinking?"

"Maybe stick with golf. But if I catch you wearing any of those really ugly golf pants, we're going to have a talk."

"Deal."

Ben eased the car into a parking space, the same one where he'd parked his old Volvo the last time he'd been here. Had it really been less than two weeks since he'd first met Holly?

"So how are we playing this?" he asked after he'd switched off the engine and turned to her. "Are you my wife again?"

"Might as well stick with the original story, right?" She fished into her purse and pulled out the big fake ring she'd donned the first time they'd played this game.

Ben plucked it from her hand. "May I?"

"Be my guest." She stuck out her left hand with a flourish, and Ben slipped the ring on. He didn't let go of her hand, though.

"So as your husband, I'm allowed to hold your hand in the store."

"Why not?"

"And maybe kiss you?"

She smiled. "I suppose that's part of the act."

"And I should probably pat your ass or grab your—"

"Okay, now you're just pushing your luck." She shoved open the car door and got out, and she was still laughing as she leaned back down to peer in at him. "Nice Mercedes, by the way."

"Thanks. Nice bra, by the way." He nodded to where her shirt gaped open. "Blue lace. I like it."

"You're hopeless," she said without venom as she slammed the car door and started toward the store.

Ben caught up with her in a few quick strides, and she took his arm without any hesitation. He caught the front door and pulled it open, gesturing her ahead of him. "Ladies first," he said as he held the door for her.

"Thank you, honey."

"My pleasure, snookiebuns."

She rolled her eyes at him, but didn't resist when he caught her hand in his and pulled her closer. It felt good having her by his side, and not just for the arm-candy effect his father seemed to feel was important. He liked spending time with her and enjoying her company beyond what she could do for his career.

He gave her hand a squeeze and looked around the store. "Let's see," he said. "Where were we the other day?"

From across the room, he saw the saleswoman he'd met with on his last visit. He watched her eyes light up, and she nearly tripped over her own feet hustling to greet them at the front of the store.

"Guess she's eager to get that commission," Ben murmured.

"She's eager to get something, all right," Holly murmured back.

"Well hello again!" the woman gushed. "My, my, that's a wonderful color on you. Really brings out your eyes." She touched Ben's shirtsleeve, ignoring Holly completely. If Holly hadn't pointed out the woman's barracuda brand of flirtation the last time they were here, Ben wasn't sure he would have noticed it.

But he was noticing it now, from the hungry way the woman looked at him, to the dagger glares she kept shooting at Holly. Ben put his arm around Holly, not sure if he was doing it to take charge of the situation or to feel Holly pressed warm and lush against him. Did it matter?

He extended his free hand to the saleswoman. "Good to see you again, Gloria," he said, reading her name off the tag she wore pinned to her blouse. "I hope you've had a wonderful week?"

"Yes, it's been—nice," she said, returning Ben's handshake by gripping his hand in both of hers. "It's so good to see you again. And your wife, too, of course."

"Yes, well, Holly here wanted to make sure we came back," he said. "I thought it would be just as easy to hit another furniture store closer to home, but she insisted you'd been so helpful to us before, so we needed to make sure you got your commission."

"Oh, well—" The woman turned to Holly and studied her with a renewed warmth. "That's very sweet of you."

"I try," Holly said. "My husband's the real charmer in the family, though."

"Yes, I can see that." The saleswoman looked back at Ben, eyeing him with curiosity. "You seem a little different than the first time you were here."

"There's a slow burn to my charm," Ben supplied. "Sort of like the boiling point of glycerin at 554 degrees Fahrenheit. Or sulfur at 823. Or—"

"Right," Gloria said, turning back to Holly. "So what is it you're looking for today?"

"Ben needs a bed. I mean—we both need a bed, of course. We share the same bed, obviously."

Ben watched her cheeks flush, surprised to see her so rattled by the flub. He tightened his arm around her, remembering how she'd come to his aid here just a few days ago. It was his turn to be the rescuer.

"Aw, look at you getting all flustered." He planted a kiss on her temple. "It's okay, sweetie. No need to be embarrassed. I'm sure it's familiar territory for Gloria."

Holly looked up at him, slate-flecked eyes wide and perplexed. "What?"

"There's nothing to be ashamed of," he said. "I'm sure Gloria's seen it plenty of times."

"Seen what?" Gloria asked, her expression eager.

"Ever since all that *Fifty Shades of Gray* business, I'm sure you've seen dozens of couples with an urgent need for a new bed," Ben said, squeezing Holly a little tighter. "Maybe the handcuffs broke the slats on the headboard, or maybe they just need something with a little more room for—well, for some of their new experiences. Am I right?"

Ben felt Holly's hand snake into his back pocket and pinch his butt cheek hard. But Gloria was nodding with such enthusiasm she didn't seem to notice the way he jumped.

"Yes!" she cried. "I can't tell you how much I've seen that lately. And I wish I had a nickel for every time I've caught a customer snaking a necktie through the headboard slats to make sure there's enough room to tie someone up."

"Really?" Holly looked at Ben, her expression more intrigued than horrified.

He touched his own necktie, stroking a finger over the silk. He almost hadn't worn one, but if he was here to play the assertive, take-charge CEO, the tie seemed like a necessary part of the costume. Holly's gaze drifted over his fingers and he wondered what she was thinking. She squirmed a little beneath his arm, then nestled closer.

"Come on," Gloria said. "Let me show you some of our sturdier models of bed frames and mattresses. I have some pieces I think the two of you will really enjoy."

She winked at Holly, then turned and marched toward the other end of the store. Ben glanced down at Holly, who rolled her eyes at him.

"Seriously?" she hissed, ducking out from under his arm. "Now we're bondage fanatics?"

"What?" he whispered back. "You wanted me to be more assertive. Surely an assertive guy would tie you to the headboard on a regular basis?"

"If Christian Gray is going to be your model for CEO behavior, I think you seriously need to rethink your plan."

"You, my dear, are most definitely not Anastasia."

Her eyes widened as she stepped around a desk, her body pressing closer to his as she moved. "Don't tell me you saw *Fifty Shades of Gray*."

"Of course not. I read the books. Well, the first one,

anyway. I wanted to see what was getting women all hot and bothered."

"And what did you figure out?"

"That in addition to not using the book as a model of CEO behavior, I probably shouldn't use it for sex tips, either."

She snorted, then hurried to catch up with Gloria. "And once again, you win the smart guy points."

"Those seem to be doing a lot for me lately."

"Here we are," Gloria announced, pivoting in front of a massive four-poster monstrosity with towering hardwood pillars. It was stained a dark red hue that was almost black, and it glistened beneath the showroom lights. Gloria grabbed hold of one of the pillars and gave it a good shake. "This is one of the sturdiest models we carry."

Ben looped an arm around Holly again, taking a scenic detour long enough to graze her ass with his palm. "It's beautiful. What can you tell us about it?"

"This is our Hillman bed in a California king. It's solid mahogany with a floating latticework headboard, tapered posts supporting the luxurious canopy. It's done in a Chinese-Chippendale fashion with solid nickel hardware and a top-of-the-line Tempurpedic mattress set."

"I like the drawers underneath," Holly said, nudging one with the toe of her shoe.

"Absolutely. Plenty of storage space for sweaters or books or—well, I'm sure you two can come up with plenty of things to store under there." She gave Holly a knowing look, and Ben did his best to look like a man who might have a full arsenal of whips and handcuffs requiring their own storage space.

"Are there matching nightstands?" he asked.

"Certainly. There's also a matching chest of drawers and a lovely armoire you can see right over there."

"What do you think, honey?" Ben turned to Holly, who

was surveying the bed with obvious fascination. "How do you like it?"

Holly reached out and pressed a hand into the mattress. "Very nice. It seems a little firm, though."

"It does feel that way, doesn't it?" Ben murmured and watched the tips of Holly's ears turn pink.

"Oh, I'm sure you'll find it's just perfect if you lie down on it," Gloria said. She bounced her palms against the mattress a couple times in illustration. "Would you like to try it out?"

Ben turned to Holly. "How about it, honey? Want to lie down with me?"

Holly looked up at him, her eyes bright and beautiful and a little wild. "Yes, please."

...

Holly eased herself down on the bed, conscious of the fact that Ben was doing the same thing on the opposite side. This was probably a bad idea, but she couldn't recall exactly why. She could feel his weight moving the mattress beneath her, and the scent of his aftershave was making her dizzy with desire. His body was big and hard and warm and so close she could reach out and touch him.

"Heavenly, isn't it?"

Gloria beamed down at her, and Holly remembered why reaching out and touching Ben probably wasn't a good idea right now.

"Yes, it's very nice," she agreed, stretching up to grab a pillow. Ben reached for it at the same time, and his fingers brushed hers, making all the nerves in her arm sizzle.

He smiled and let go of the pillow and grabbed her hand instead. He gave a soft squeeze she knew was probably meant to be comforting, but it just left her thinking about how badly she wanted his hands all over her body.

"What do you think, honey?" he asked. "Could you see us sleeping together in this every night?"

God, yes. Sleeping and kissing and touching and—

"No!" She hadn't meant to say the word out loud, and she felt idiotic for doing it. But her brain had latched tightly to her own memory of happily-ever-after fantasies and how that whole mess had turned out last time.

Ben was giving her a perplexed look, so Holly softened her voice and tried again. "I just mean I can't picture it yet, because we're on the wrong sides. That's my side of the bed, remember?"

"Right, of course," Ben said, grinning as he rolled closer. "Let's fix that."

He moved over the top of her, and Holly felt her breath catch in her throat. His hand brushed the edge of her breast as she scooted out of the way, moving into the spot that was still warm from his body heat.

"Better?" he asked.

"Much." Holly licked her lips, trying to get some air in her lungs. She saw Ben's gaze fall to her mouth, and he shifted a little on the bed. His leg bumped hers, sending another pulse of electricity through her body. He let go of her hand and slid his palm to her hip. It was an innocent enough gesture, and totally in character for a supposedly married couple out bed shopping on a Saturday afternoon.

So why did it leave her breathless with the urge to take off her clothes?

"Does it come in other finishes?" Ben asked. "I like this color, but my wife tends to prefer lighter hues."

"You know, that's an excellent question," Gloria said. "The cherry has been our most popular option, but we just got a new catalog yesterday. I haven't even opened it yet, but I can go take a look to see if they've released some new finishes."

"That would be great," Ben said, his hand still on Holly's

hip.

She watched as Gloria scurried away, conscious of Ben's chest mere inches from her face. She could feel his breath rustling her hair, and the curve of his palm around her hip left his fingers grazing the edge of her backside.

"How am I doing?"

Holly blinked and turned her attention back to Ben. "What?"

"With my charming, assertive CEO persona?" He lifted his hand from her hip and reached up to brush a strand of hair from her cheek, his eyes dancing with amusement. He rested his hand on the bed between them, leaving Holly aching for his touch. "Am I pulling it off effectively?"

"Oh. Yes, yes of course." She'd almost forgotten the reason for their visit. Right, she was supposed to be coaching him. She'd do that any minute now. If she could just stop thinking about his leg brushing hers, the swell of his bicep under that gloriously soft shirt, the zipper on his trousers that would be so easy to tug down and—

"Any tips?" he asked. "Anything you want me to be doing that I'm not?"

Touching me. Kissing me. Stroking me.

"No. I think you're nailing it." She swallowed hard, trying to regain her composure. "You've definitely improved your CEO charisma."

"I'm not laying it on too thick?"

"Nope. Not too thick. Not at all."

God, she sounded like a moron. She should come up with something intelligent to say. "You're doing a great job holding eye contact. With Gloria, I mean."

"And with you."

She wasn't sure if it was a question or a statement, but she nodded anyway. "Yes. With me."

"I've been trying to work on it. I never noticed how much

I avoided eye contact until you pointed it out."

His gaze was locked on hers, unblinking. She knew he probably didn't mean to give her a smoldering look, but that's what it felt like. Chemistry, is that what he'd called it? Whatever it was crackling between them was making Holly dizzy.

"Your posture has been perfect, too," she said. "I mean, not right now—"

"No, probably not at the moment." He smiled. "I can't recall you giving me any tips on how a CEO should conduct himself on a bed."

"Right. Um, I think you're doing pretty well figuring it out on your own."

She could feel her hands shaking as liquid heat pooled in her belly and moved down. She wanted him to touch her again. She *needed* him to touch her again.

"Thanks for the feedback," Ben said. "You know, I think there's one more thing I could be doing to solidify our ruse and really demonstrate my assertiveness."

"What's that?"

"This."

Ben threaded his fingers into her hair and pulled her close, his lips finding hers. He kissed her softly at first, then with more intensity as his knee brushed hers and his hand slid from her hair to the nape of her neck.

Holly moaned and kissed him back, her palm finding its place in the hollow of his chest. His mouth was warm and soft and he was kissing her so exquisitely she couldn't see straight. She closed her eyes and slipped two fingers between the buttons on his shirt, aching to feel his skin against her fingertips.

He made a sound low in his throat and deepened the kiss. His palm slid lower, brushing the side of her breast, the dip in her waist, the curve of her hip—

"Looks like it comes in honey!"

Holly jerked back, breaking the kiss and possibly Ben's

eyeglasses. "Who comes in honey?"

He reached up to adjust his glasses as Gloria skimmed a finger over a page in her catalog. She kept her gaze down for a few more beats, and Holly said a silent thank you—for her discretion or her cluelessness, she wasn't quite sure. Holly leaned back to put a little space between her and Ben, but she could still feel him everywhere.

"The bed," Gloria said. "In addition to the cherry finish, the manufacturer just started making it in honey. Here's a sample."

She held out the catalog, and Ben leaned forward to peer at the picture. His shoulder brushed her breast, and Holly nearly bolted off the bed as a fresh wave of pleasure coursed through her.

"It's beautiful," he said. "What do you think, dear?"

"I think it's amazing."

"Shall we do it?"

She looked at him, half expecting to see a teasing glint in his eye. But there was nothing teasing in his expression. She saw a flicker of her own reflection in his glasses, and she realized she wore the same look of desire she was seeing now in his gaze.

Something clicked inside her. She was done fighting it. All her energy was consumed with wanting him, and she didn't have the strength to keep pretending otherwise. So what if this wouldn't last? She wasn't living in the future. She was living in the present. And she wanted him *now*.

"Yes," Holly said, taking a deep breath. "We should do it."

Ben nodded, his gaze locked on hers. "Are you sure?"

"Positive." Her voice sounded breathy and high, and she wasn't entirely sure they were talking about the same thing. But she was about to find out.

"Give her your credit card," she said. "And let's get out of here."

Chapter Twelve

It didn't take Holly long to get the answer to her question, mostly because Ben had the wherewithal to ask on his own.

"Just to be clear, are you suggesting we have sex?" One massive palm gripped the steering wheel as he merged onto the freeway.

The other hand caressed her knee, sending goose bumps up Holly's leg. She nodded, too turned on to speak, only dimly aware that he probably couldn't see the gesture with his gaze fixed on the road.

"I just want to be sure," he said. "Because I don't always pick up on all the social cues, so I want to be absolutely, positively certain—"

"Yes," Holly said, surprised by the breathlessness in her own voice. "I want you, you want me, and I'm tired of fighting it. Take the next exit, please."

"Where are we going?" His hand moved a fraction of an inch up her thigh, and Holly nearly moaned with pleasure.

"You don't have a bed, and my place is too far away. There's a hotel right up there and it seems like the surest way to have you inside me within five minutes."

"Yes, ma'am." He grinned and slid his hand further up her thigh. "And this is why you're well-qualified to coach me on assertiveness. You're a woman who knows what she wants."

"I think you've mastered a few things yourself, Mr. CEO." She watched his hand slide further up her thigh as he pushed her skirt up higher.

"Yes, but a little hands-on experience is always valuable if I'm really going to get behind the issue for some strategic interplay."

She grinned, pretty sure this was the first time anyone had attempted to use business jargon as a seduction tool. "I think I can slot you in."

"Excellent. I'd like to touch base on the liquidity of your assets as soon as possible."

He shoved her skirt higher and Holly let her legs fall apart. Ben accepted the invitation, his fingers grazing the satin center of her panties, and Holly heard herself gasp.

"God yes!" she gasped, pressing against his fingertips. "Right there."

Ben smiled, his gaze still on the road, his fingers slipping beneath the elastic of her panties. She felt him dip inside her and knew from the way his finger slid and glided that she was already slick with desire. That he'd been the one to make her that way. His moan confirmed it.

"God, you're wet," he said. "Take these off."

She didn't need to be told twice. She looped her fingers under the elastic at her hips, yanking the panties off and tossing them into her purse at her feet. Ben wasted no time claiming her again, his fingers slipping inside her as he steered the car onto the off-ramp. One hand worked the turn signal. The other worked Holly's clit, circling and stroking until she cried out with pleasure.

She threw her head back against the seat, aching to have

more than his fingers inside her this time. She pressed against his hand, forcing his digits deeper as he screeched into the parking lot of a high-rise hotel.

Ben braked in a parking spot, then drew his hand back and kissed her hard. "Wait here," he said as he undid his seat belt.

Holly nodded and crossed her legs as he threw open the car door and sprinted for the hotel lobby. She watched him go, smoothing her hair down with hands that wouldn't stop shaking. She barely had time to undo her own seat belt before Ben was back at the car and yanking her door open. "Come on. We've got a room on the eighth floor, which means I can use the elevator ride to get most of your clothes off."

She let him pull her to her feet, electrified by his touch. They raced to the hotel's side door, pulling each other along as they headed for the bank of elevators.

"This way." Ben gripped her hand tighter as he pulled her into the elevator after him and hit the button for the eighth floor. Then he turned and pushed her up against the wall. "Where were we?" he murmured.

"You were kissing me. And touching me. And using business jargon to get me hot."

"Right. I think I was dipping my pen in the company ink."

"Christ, yes," she gasped as his hand found its way under her skirt again, and Holly thanked her lucky stars she hadn't bothered putting her panties back on. His fingers slipped inside her as she braced herself on the handrail. Her palms were damp with sweat and she lost her grip, but Ben held her up, pinning her against the wall. He was completely in control, just like she'd coached him.

She was equally thrilled and terrified.

"Is this what they mean by market penetration?" she groaned as his fingers slid deep inside her.

"Absolutely," he said as he slid his finger out and then in

again. "We need to really drill down on the issue."

"I believe it requires some deep analysis."

Holly let go of the rail to caress one hand up his back. The other hand found its way to the front of his trousers and she moaned aloud at the hardness she found there. "Are your assets expanding, or are you just happy to see me?"

"I'm really fucking happy to see you," he breathed against her neck as he kissed her there, then worked his way down. "God, Holly, I want you. I want to taste you and touch you and feel myself sliding inside you."

"I accept that offer." Everything inside her buzzed with energy, and she almost couldn't believe she was about to have him for real.

The elevator doors swished open, and Ben stepped in front of her, shielding her from prying eyes. She smoothed her hands over her hair, nodding to the elderly couple that stood frowning beside the elevator. Ben turned and grabbed her hand, pulling her along behind him.

"Sir. Ma'am," he said. "Lovely afternoon."

Holly stifled a giggle as he tugged her down the hall. She could hear the old woman tittering behind her.

"Did you see that—"

The words faded behind them as Ben shoved the key card into the slot on the door. He pushed it open, then took off his glasses. Tossing them on a table by the door, he turned back to Holly. He didn't bother with lights as he pulled her inside, kicking the door shut behind them.

"Are you up for some collaborative interface?"

"I should be able to fit you in and seal the deal for good."

Her voice was high and tight and she was running out of business jargon and working brain cells. She twined her fingers around his neck as their mouths collided in a kiss so fierce it uncoiled something dark and primal inside her. Ben walked her backward toward the bed, holding her upright and not breaking the kiss as his hands moved over her back, her ribs, her neck.

Holly felt the back of her legs bump the bed as his hands moved to her hips. Then he cupped her ass, and she gave a squeak of surprise as he lifted her off the ground and tossed her back onto the bed. He fell with her, pinning her beneath all that lovely, solid weight.

He broke the kiss to gaze into her eyes. "Last chance. You sure?"

"Positive. Kiss me again."

"I'll take direction from you any day." He claimed her mouth as she clawed at his shirt, tugging it free from his pants. She slid her palms over his newly bared flesh, enjoying the flex of muscle in his lower back. Ben was still kissing her silly, his mouth exploring the edge of her jawbone, the tip of her chin, the soft hollow behind her ear. One of his hands slipped beneath her, unhooking her bra through her shirt as though he'd done it a million times before. She moaned as her breasts slipped free of the underwire, and his palm slid around to cup one, his thumb grazing her nipple.

Holly clutched at his belt, needing more. She wanted to feel his skin against hers, to know the intimate weight of his chest pressing her into the bedspread. She skimmed her hands up his body, bringing them to rest on his chest. She pushed against him, and Ben broke the kiss. She seized the chance to grab hold of his tie, her fingers fumbling with the knot at the top.

"The downside of being a CEO," he murmured, laughing as she tugged at the necktie in frustration. "It takes a lot less effort to remove pajama pants."

"I'm about two seconds from chewing through this damn tie."

"Allow me."

Ben worked the knot free while Holly marveled at how

quickly he'd managed to master the unfamiliar accessory. The man was a fast learner, she had to admit. She reached up and began slipping buttons through their holes, stripping him down to a plain white undershirt. He tossed his tie aside and went back to kissing her, marking a burning path of lip prints down her throat and into the hollow between her breasts. Holly shoved the sleeves of his dress shirt off his shoulders, her fingertips lingering on the curve of his biceps.

He had her skirt hiked up over her hips again, and she wrapped her legs around him, pressing herself into the bulge in the front of his slacks. She arched her hips to grind against him, wanting more.

Ben drew back again, angling himself up on his forearms. "How about we expedite negotiations with some synergistic processing?"

"Say what?"

He grinned. "Let's take our shirts off on the count of three."

"Deal."

"Three, two —"

Holly yanked her top off, not willing to wait the extra second. She tossed the garment aside and shrugged off her bra, thrilled to see Ben shirtless and gloriously bare-chested before her.

"Very efficient," she said. "The mark of a good CEO."

"You should see what I can do with a spreadsheet."

She laughed as his lips found hers again and his bare chest pressed against hers. He had a light dusting of chest hair, and the feel of it against her nipples was exquisite. She moved her hands down his back, savoring every inch of muscle and bone as Ben kissed his way down her throat and between her breasts. His mouth found her nipple and Holly cried out.

"God, that feels good."

"You have the most beautiful nipples in the world,"

he said, making a trail of kisses from one to the other. "So sensitive."

She gripped the back of his head as he continued to lick and suck and stroke until she was nearly mindless. When she was sure she couldn't take it anymore, she struggled to sit up, pushing him onto his back as she moved.

"I need you inside me," she said, reaching for the front of his slacks and unhooking the button. She grabbed the tab of his zipper and tugged down. It caught halfway down, refusing to budge. She gave it another tug. Nothing. She let out a small scream of frustration.

"No! This isn't happening."

He laughed and moved her hands aside, his own fingers replacing hers on his fly. "I've got this," he said, and yanked it open with maddening ease.

"How did you—"

"I've been honing my skills at both dressing and undressing myself."

"A man in charge," she said, moving down his body and taking his pants and boxer briefs with her. "I like it."

"I know you do. Maybe I should get a gold star."

"Absolutely."

"And a blowjob."

"Your wish is my command," she said with a laugh, refusing to let her brain go down the path of the last time she'd allowed herself to be at the beck and call of a career-driven man. That was then, and this was now, and she urgently wanted to live in the now.

"God, yes," he said as Holly crawled back up his body, admiring the gorgeous, naked length of it. She took hold of his cock and used the tip of her tongue to make a slow circle around the head of it. Ben groaned as she flattened her tongue and drew him all the way into her mouth. She released the pressure, letting him slide all the way out before drawing him back in again.

"This would work better as a collaborative assimilation," he said.

She licked the tip of his cock, grinning. "I don't know what that means, but I'll agree to pretty much anything you suggest at this point."

His hand closed around her ankle and tugged. Holly giggled as his other hand slid to her hip and he pulled her gently around so she faced the other way. She had one knee on either side of his head, and her whole body hovering over his as she knelt on all fours. For an instant, she felt self-conscious. Then she felt nothing but pleasure as Ben's tongue dipped inside her.

"Oh, God."

She peered between her breasts and thighs to see him smiling as he teased and stroked and made her mindless with his tongue. Realizing she still had a death-grip on his cock, Holly focused her attention there once more, drawing him into her mouth.

Ben moaned, and the vibration of it sent a buzz of pleasure coursing through her. He continued probing her with his tongue, making slow circles around her clit as Holly sucked him in deep, hopeful he felt even a fraction of the pleasure he was giving her. They stayed like that until Holly felt her knees start to quiver. She was on the brink, and she could tell he was, too.

"Holly, stop," he gasped, his breath warm on her thigh. "I need to be inside you."

"Condom," she breathed, thankful she'd had the foresight to shove one in her wallet. She located her purse on the floor and found the foil packet in a heartbeat. She tore it open and sheathed him with it faster than she'd ever performed the task in her life. Then she moved over him, pinning him on his back. She crawled up his body until her knees were splayed around his hips and his cock was poised so close to her opening, even the tiniest movement would have him inside her. Ben put his hands on her waist.

"Do it, Holly," he breathed. "Fuck me."

The words sent a jolt of pleasure through her body, rattling her from the nape of her neck to the tips of her toes. He was staking his claim, stepping up to the plate like a real CEO and demanding what he wanted.

And what he wanted was *her*.

Holly licked her lips. "You drive a hard bargain, Mr. CEO."

"Let's put this deal to bed."

"I'm nothing if not a team player."

She grabbed hold of his cock and slid it inside her, gasping as he filled her completely. She stayed motionless for a few seconds, her body adjusting to the feel of him rooted so deeply. Then she began to move.

He moaned and slid his hands up her rib cage, cupping her breasts as she moved over him.

"Ben, you feel so good."

"So do you. So tight. So wet."

She rode him slowly at first, enjoying the slow build of pleasure and the feel of his swollen shaft buried deep inside her. She felt her hips quickening even before she realized she was doing it, her pace growing more frenzied as the pressure inside her began to build.

"That's it, baby," he murmured, stroking his thumbs over her nipples. "Make yourself come."

She drew her hands up to her breasts, her fingers twining with his to squeeze and knead and stroke. She wasn't usually this bold when it came to touching herself in front of a man, but something about Ben brought it out in her. Emboldened by the pleasure coursing through her, she moved her palm down her belly. She let her index finger graze her clit, softly at first, then with a firmer touch.

She gasped at the sensation as Ben thrust his hips up to drive deeper into her. "That's it, honey," he whispered. "Show me how you like it."

She'd never felt so bold with a man before, so confident taking her own pleasure while a strong, solid male moved beneath her.

"God, Ben."

"Keep going, baby. Stroke your clit while you ride me."

"That feels so fucking good," she moaned.

"Tell me when you're close, baby."

"I'm close," she breathed, riding him harder now. "So close."

"Open your eyes, Holly. I want to watch you when you come."

She obeyed, pretty sure she'd do anything he told her to right now. His eyes were dark and molten, the amber flecks sparking in a beam of light through a part in the curtains. Holly locked her gaze on his, conscious of the blood pounding in her head, Ben pounding between her legs, and the delicious eruption building inside her.

"Ben!"

"Yes," he groaned. "Do it. I'm there with you."

He thrust up to meet her, angling his hips to hit something so mind-blowing she went orbiting into a new dimension of pleasure. She screamed from the shock and the ecstasy and the utter certainty she'd never felt anything like this before.

She saw Ben's eyes go wide and felt him shudder beneath her. "Oh, God."

His gaze locked with hers as he dropped his hands to her hips and brought her down harder onto him. With each wave that hit her, another crashed into him until they were both sweaty and dizzy and totally, completely spent.

Holly collapsed forward, landing with her head on his

chest. Ben rolled to his side, easing her with him so they lay face to face with their breath mingling and their limbs caught in a delicious tangle.

"Well," he said. "That was the best internal business merger I've ever been part of."

...

Ben didn't remember falling asleep with Holly in his arms, but it must have happened at some point. He woke bleary-eyed and confused about why his pants were hanging from the lamp and why they seemed to be vibrating.

It took him a few seconds to realize his phone was ringing. As gently as he could, he eased Holly off his chest and rolled away from her. He burrowed a hand into his pants pocket and pulled out the phone, peering at the readout. Where the hell were his glasses?

The words came into focus as he squinted, and Ben felt his gut sink.

Dad.

He thought about not answering it. Then he remembered the lecture Lyle had given two days before.

"A good CEO never takes a break," he'd insisted. "Your mind's always working, your guard's always up, and your phone's always on."

Ben sighed and hit the button to answer the call. "Hey, Dad. What's up?"

"I've been trying to reach you for an hour. Where the hell have you been?"

"I, uh—was in the middle of a performance evaluation."

"You've gotta shove that off on human resources," Lyle grumbled. "You've got more important things to do."

Ben looked down at Holly sleeping beside him and couldn't think of anything in the world more important. As though feeling his gaze on her, she stirred and opened her eyes. Her lashes fluttered and she smiled at him, and Ben felt his heart lurch in his chest.

"Right," Ben said, already forgetting whatever the hell they were discussing.

"I got a call from Kleinberger."

That got Ben's attention. "What did they say?"

"They want to sign the deal. They're willing to move fast, too."

"Wow." Ben raked his fingers through his hair, surprised at the surge of pride rushing through him. He'd had a hand in landing that deal. Not just from the engineering side, either, but as a real, honest-to-God, hobnobbing CEO. He sat up a little straighter on the edge of the bed and smiled at Holly. She smiled back, making his heart stumble against his ribs.

"That's great, Dad. Congratulations."

Ben paused to see if his father might congratulate him, but Lyle just grunted. "Yeah, it's terrific. Look, we need to wine and dine these guys. Really seal the deal, if you know what I mean. Remember that party we threw last year when Jolen Brothers signed on?"

Ben remembered. He'd been dragged out of the engineering dungeon and ordered to make charming conversation with Jolen executives. He'd ended up spending the whole night by the canapés chatting with the server about her husband's desire to return to college for an advanced degree in economics.

"Yes, I remember," he said. "Are you wanting to do something similar?"

"No, bigger. I told Molly to get in touch with that event planner we used for that bullshit charity thing last fall. We're going to pull out all the stops for this one. They're even flying the company founder out here to nail down the final details in person."

Holly yawned and stretched, then leaned up to plant a soft kiss on his forehead. He drew back, weirdly uncomfortable having a beautiful, naked woman touch him while his dad yammered on about due diligence and monetized assets. He squeezed her hand, then rolled off the bed and reached for his underwear, pulling them on while she watched.

He shuffled across the room, gripping the phone with one hand while he located his glasses with the other. "That sounds like a good plan," he said. "Do you want me to prepare a speech?"

Ben couldn't believe he'd just offered that, nor could he believe Lyle's response. "Yeah, I think that would be good. The Kleinberger guys like you. Throw something together that'll dazzle them."

"Dazzle. I can do that." He ambled back to the bedside and grabbed his pants. He stepped into them while Holly sat up and pulled the sheet over her breasts. Her hair was tousled and her cheeks were flushed from sleep or beard burn or some combination of both, and he wanted her all over again. He started to reach for her, but his father's voice stopped him in his tracks.

"Make sure you bring a date. That hot little number you had the other night should do the trick."

"Hot little number," Ben repeated, looking at Holly. "I should be able to pull that off."

"Good. Look, I've gotta run. The party's next Saturday. Try to have all our ducks in a row by then. And Ben?"

"Yeah?"

"Don't screw this up."

Lyle disconnected the call, and Ben stood holding the phone for a minute. It was hardly the afterglow he'd been savoring in his dreams just a few minutes ago. He shoved the phone in his pocket and sat down on the bed beside Holly.

"Let me guess," she said, resting a hand on his thigh.

"Your dad?"

"Yep. Sounds like we got the Kleinberger deal."

"Really? Ben, that's amazing!" She threw her arms around his neck and kissed him, her softness enveloping him all over again. "Congratulations," she murmured against his neck. "I'm so proud of you."

The words hit him right in the spleen and his chest flooded with an odd mix of pride and sadness. Would it have killed his father to say the same five words?

But Holly had said them, and that counted for a lot. "Are you free next Saturday?" he asked.

"I can check. Why?"

"We're throwing a big party for the Kleinberger execs. My dad wants you to come with me."

Holly drew back and gave him a salacious grin. "I just did."

Ben laughed, and for a moment, he forgot all the awkward, lingering feelings about his dad. He kissed her on the mouth, then reached for the edge of the sheet. "He called you a hot little number," he said as he tugged down the sheet and claimed her breast with his mouth. Holly twined her fingers in his hair and arched against him. He cupped her other breast in his palm, taking his time to work his way between one and the other.

"Hot little number?" She giggled, which came out sounding partly like a moan. "What is this, 1958?"

"In my dad's mind, yes. He also might be under the impression that you're my girlfriend instead of my branding consultant."

"Oh really?" Her tone was teasing, but Ben felt her pull back just a little.

"Yep." He sat up and planted a kiss at the edge of her jaw, then another right below her earlobe. "The thing is, I don't think that's such a bad idea."

"The party? Well, I can check my schedule, but—"

"No, the girlfriend thing." He drew back and looked at her, hoping to see her eyes light up. There was no reaction, but maybe he just hadn't been clear enough.

Be bold. Say what you really want.

"How about it, Holly?" he asked, leaning down to kiss her shoulder. "What do you say we take a shot at a real relationship?"

He let those words hang between them for a moment as he kissed his way from her shoulder along her collarbone, then drew back to study her face.

She wasn't smiling.

Okay, so "girlfriend" was a big word to start throwing around. He maybe could have eased in more gently or started by asking her out on a date.

But wasn't it Holly who'd encouraged him to be assertive? To listen to his inner voice and speak his mind? His inner voice was yelling at him to go for it, to stand up and tell her how he felt.

Apparently, Holly's inner voice was telling her something very different. Like *"run."*

"Ben, I don't think that's such a good idea," she said slowly. "If you need me there as your PR coach, I'm up to the task."

"That's actually not what I need from you," he said, trying not to feel stung by the rejection. "I need you by my side for this event. I want you to be my rock, my support system, my partner, my—"

"Arm candy?"

"Sure," he said, surprised to see her flinch at the word. "We've joked about that before. You're a beautiful woman, and it doesn't hurt—either my ego or my image—to have you by my side. Is that so wrong?"

She shook her head and stood up fast, grabbing her bra

from the floor at the foot of the bed. She tried to yank it on, but ended up whacking herself in the nose with the strap. Still she didn't meet his eyes.

"I've played your doting wife already, Ben. When the need suited your career, I did that and you paid me for it. It was a job."

"A job," he repeated, trying to understand what she was telling him.

"Yes, a job. And now that you've landed the Kleinberger deal, my work here is done."

Ben blinked, trying to keep up with the conversation as she jerked her top on, fumbling with the buttons. She still wouldn't look at him, but he could have sworn he caught a shimmer of tears in the corner of her eye.

"I'm not talking about work," he said. "I'm talking about the two of us hanging out together because we enjoy each other's company outside business."

"There's no *us* outside business, Ben—don't you see?"

"I don't. We've laughed together and played together and made crazy passionate love together, and as far as I can tell, you enjoyed all of those things."

"I did. I *do*. But I just don't—I mean I can't—God, where are my shoes?"

"Holly, sit down for a minute."

He wasn't sure if she'd obey, but he wasn't surprised when she did. She dropped onto the edge of the bed, a good two feet of space between them. Ben suspected she'd prefer to keep it that way.

She was quiet a moment, and he watched her take a few deep breaths. When she turned to face him, her odd lavender-hued eyes were glittery. "Look, Ben—I took this job because I needed the money."

"Okay," he said slowly. "I'll have the second half of it to you by end-of-business tomorrow."

"Thank you." She pressed her lips together and looked down at her hands.

He watched her, trying to figure out what had her so undone. He got the sense there was more to her money woes than the need to pay off an Office Max credit card. Softening his tone, he probed again. "Do you mind telling me why you needed the money so urgently?"

She sighed and folded her hands together in her lap, her gaze still fixed on them instead of on his face. "When I bought the building that's home to First Impressions, I made a stupid mistake."

"You mean like a balloon mortgage or something?"

"Worse. I co-signed with my husband. Ex-husband, I mean, but we were married at the time. It was idiotic and stupid and—"

"Hey," he said, reaching out to touch her hand. "It's not that dumb. A lot of married people sign loans together. It's part of the partnership."

"Partnership," she scoffed, shaking her head a little. "There was no partnership to the arrangement. He resented my career from the very beginning, and I should have known better. I made a mistake." She sighed. "Anyway, that's why I needed to take this job with you. To get out from under that loan and refinance in my name alone."

Ben let the words wash over him, trying to make sense of what she was telling him. He dropped his hand back onto the bed, not sure he felt right touching her. So it was all about the money all along. He'd known that, on some level—he'd signed the damn check himself. But still, he'd hoped it was evolving into more. Had he been naive?

"So this whole time, I was just a paycheck?" he said slowly. "A chance to save your real estate investment?"

She looked up at him, alarm flashing in her eyes. He waited for her to argue, to tell him he was wrong and that it had become so much more than that to her.

But instead, she shook her head. "I would hope you think I earned that money," she said. "Every penny of it. I worked hard for you."

"I'm not questioning that. But this whole job was just another business transaction for you."

Again, he waited for her to argue. He stayed silent, wanting to hear her say those words. She didn't speak for a long time, so Ben reached out again and touched her hand once more. "I wanted a shot at a real relationship with you. Something real. Something meaningful."

Was it his imagination, or did she flinch?

She looked at him long and hard. Then she looked away. "Yes." He watched her throat move as she swallowed. "To answer your question, it was always just a business arrangement."

The words hit him like a punch to the gut. "Nothing more?"

"Nothing more." She looked down at the comforter, plucking at a loose thread. "I'm sorry, Ben. Our careers and our personal lives have gotten too tangled up together and I think it's time we said good-bye."

He stared at her. Would an alpha male CEO catch her by the hand and ask her to stay? Would he demand she sit here and listen to all the reasons they should give this thing a shot? He started to open his mouth, then stopped.

She looked at him then, and the sadness in her eyes told him everything he needed to know. Her mind was made up. If she was really ready to walk away from this, maybe she wasn't the woman he thought she was.

You're just like your father after all. Relationships can never turn out to be more than career-building tools.

As if to emphasize the point, Holly stood up and smoothed her hands down her skirt. She took a step away from the bed, and the look on her face nearly broke his heart.

"Good-bye, Ben," she said, and took another step back. Then another, her gaze still on his face like she was trying to memorize him. Then she turned away and moved toward the door.

As the door clicked shut behind her, Ben took a deep breath.

Then he swallowed his alpha male ego, and let her go.

Chapter Thirteen

Ben glared at himself in the dressing room mirror. The tuxedo he wore made him look like an angry monkey, which only served to piss him off more.

"You look fabulous!"

Ben turned to see Marcus the salesman smiling at him through the open doorway. Ben pivoted and checked out his side view in the mirror, but that wasn't much better. From this angle, he looked more like a disgruntled penguin.

Marcus didn't seem to notice, or if he did, he was too discreet to say anything. "The fit is almost perfect," he said, hustling forward to straighten Ben's lapels. "A little tailoring through the shoulders and we'll have you fixed up in a jiff. When did you say this charity gala is happening?"

"Saturday."

"Perfect. We'll have you all squared away. Do you need any more ties?"

"Ties," Ben repeated. "Let me think on that." Christ, he'd bought more ties in the last month than he'd purchased in his entire life up to that point, which wasn't saying much. Still, he had no idea when he'd ever get around to wearing them all. Dinner dates with Holly?

That wasn't going to happen.

He'd tried to get up the nerve to call, but each time he heard her words echoing in his ears.

It was always just a business arrangement.

So that's how it was. He didn't know why the idea had caught him by surprise. It was how all his father's relationships had been structured, and Ben had been doing his best to master his dad's job. He was fulfilling his own destiny here.

A rustling behind him pulled Ben from his thoughts. "I think he needs one of those snot rag things."

Ben turned at the sound of his best friend's voice, and smiled to see Parker ambling toward the open dressing room.

Marcus eyed Parker and gave an uncomfortable little laugh. "Snot rag?"

"I think he's talking about a pocket square," Ben said. "And the fact that I even know what a pocket square is means I've effectively become my father."

"Pocket square! Yes, of course," Marcus said. "I have several I can show you if you'd like?"

"That'd be great," Parker told him. "It'll give me a chance to talk to this dumbass."

Marcus looked back at Ben, probably wondering if it was safe to leave the two of them alone together. Ben gave a silent nod, so Marcus turned and hurried toward the door.

"Absolutely," the salesman said, scurrying down the hall as he chattered on about silk paisley while Ben turned back to the mirror and straightened his tie.

"You know, you couldn't become your father if you had a million snot rags," Parker said, leaning against the wall. "And you couldn't be a bigger dipshit if you put catnip in your pockets and crawled into a lion's den."

"Thank you. Is this heartwarming little pep talk almost

over?"

Parker shook his head and slugged Ben in the shoulder. It was enough to make him turn around and look his friend in the eye again. "What?" Ben demanded.

"I knew you were a mess when you texted me to bail on our gym time because your dad ordered you to get a new tuxedo. Don't you have enough monkey suits?"

"Not an actual tuxedo, apparently. Who knew that was a thing?"

"It's a thing in your dad's world. It doesn't have to be in your world."

"What's that supposed to mean?"

"I mean you're the CEO now, Ben. Over the last few weeks, I've watched you turn into a corporate badass in ways that have nothing to do with your father. I've watched you land business deals and make professional contacts and give speeches that knock people's socks off. That's all you, buddy."

"It's not all me," he said, still straightening his tie for no apparent reason. The damn thing was straight as a yardstick. "I couldn't have done it without Holly."

"Holly," Parker said fondly, and Ben fixed his friend with a scowl. "Sorry about that," Parker said. "If it helps, I think she was the best thing that ever happened to you."

"Nope, doesn't help. Try again."

"I suppose it doesn't," he said. "And maybe she'll change her mind. But in the meantime, she's given you the best gift she possibly could."

"A kick in the balls? That wasn't on my Christmas list."

"No, dumbass. A chance to stand on your own two feet in the family company. With or without Holly, now's your chance to show everyone what you've got."

Ben studied his best friend, appreciating the earnestness in his expression and the truth in his words. Appreciating the fact that Parker had stood by him these last few days while he'd grumbled and snarled and done his damnedest not to think about Holly.

But Parker had a point. Now wasn't the time to think about her. It was the time to prove he could do this CEO thing, with or without her. It was time to prove he could be a leader *his* way.

Ben reached up and grabbed the edge of his tie. He hesitated a moment, thinking about his dad. Then with a quick yank, he pulled the tie out of the shirt collar. He stared at it for a moment like it was a well-used tissue.

Then he dropped it on the dressing room floor.

"In that case," Ben said. "I'll start by ditching this."

• • •

Holly paced slowly across the front of the room, pausing to rest her palm on the purple conference table before smoothing a hand down her black pencil skirt. Her posture was perfect, her voice was commanding, her mastery of the subject matter was impeccable.

The rest of her wasn't feeling so hot.

"As you can see, we've mapped out an aggressive rebranding plan for Sunstone Lemonade," she said, projecting an energy she didn't feel. "It's fresh, it's edgy, and above all, it's guaranteed to grow your business by more than fifteen percent within the first six months of campaign launch. Are there any questions?"

"I have one."

Holly turned to Miriam, the only other person in the boardroom and the only team member brave enough to sit through this dry run of her next account presentation.

"Yes?" Holly pointed at Miriam, pretending not to know her name. "Ma'am, you had a question?"

"I do. What the fuck is wrong with you?"

Holly rolled her eyes. "Come on, Miriam. I need to practice. I'm trying to nail this presentation."

"And you think that's better than nailing Ben?" Miriam shook her head, making her chandelier earrings sway like wind chimes. "You're off your game, sweetie. No offense, but it shows."

"So give me feedback. Do I need to dial up the zing in the PowerPoint slides or wear something a little more edgy?"

"You need to stop looking like someone backed over your dog with a bulldozer."

"What's that supposed to mean?"

"I mean you look miserable." Miriam sighed and leaned forward across the table. "Look, Holly—I know you're bummed about what happened with Ben. But do you think maybe you overreacted just a little?"

"No."

"Way to keep an open mind."

Holly dropped into an empty chair and kicked off the stupid stilettos that had been pinching her toes all afternoon. Belatedly, she realized she was seated in the exact chair she'd been in when Ben's presentation prompted her to strip naked in the conference room. She stood up again, feeling twitchy and annoyed.

"Look, it was never going to work," she said. "Things were doomed the second we crossed that line between business and pleasure. I should have known better than to let those two things get all mixed up together."

"That's where you're wrong," Miriam argued. "Just because Chase screwed you over at the intersection of love and money doesn't mean every guy is destined to do that."

"But he was becoming his father," she said. "Ben, I mean. The sports car, the golf game, the assertive personality—"

"Hon, guys can have those things without being raging dickheads like your ex or like Lyle Langley. That's like concluding that because Ben has testicles and Chase has testicles and Lyle has testicles—"

"Stop. I don't need this many mental pictures of testicles."

"Well you need something to slap you out of this stupid belief that there's a correlation between businessmen with a commanding presence and guys who want you to trade in your career for six inches of man meat and two feet of cable chaining you to the stove."

"It was more than six inches," Holly muttered, then shook her head. "That's beside the point."

"What is the point then?"

"I was starting to fall for him," she said softly. "The real Ben. The geeky Ben, not the schmoozy, in-charge CEO, but the *real* him. At least the him I *thought* was the real him. The one who thinks a *Star Wars* DVD is a romantic gift."

"It *was* a romantic gift."

"I know!" Holly smacked the table in frustration at her own inability to form a coherent argument. She was usually so good at this.

"You weren't just falling for the geek, though," Miriam said. "You were falling for the sexy gym rat with the commanding presence in the boardroom and the G-spot locator in his middle finger."

Holly buried her head in her hands. "Why did I tell you that?"

"And you're petrified that all these different versions of the guy can't peacefully coexist in one body."

Holly kept her head down, considering. Did Miriam have a point? She looked up to see her friend watching her with a disturbing mix of sympathy and clever calculation.

"You think he can be both," Holly said. "The geek and the powerful businessman."

"I've never met him, remember? But I do think it's possible."

Holly took a shaky breath and looked down at her hands. Had she completely blown it with Ben? Was it too late to find out?

When she looked up at Miriam, her friend wore a sympathetic expression. Holly licked her lips. "I think it's possible I love him," she said softly.

"I know it is."

Holly shook her head. "So what do I do?"

Miriam reached out and patted her hand, her lacquered red nails bright against Holly's pale skin. "I have a plan."

Chapter Fourteen

"Nice one!" Ben clapped Joe Kleinberger on the shoulder, beaming as the old man did a fist pump and turned away from the vintage Pac Man game in the corner of Ben's office.

"I can't believe I beat my high score from thirty years ago!" Kleinberger grinned. "I also can't believe you knew about my secret passion for old school arcade games."

"I saw it on your Facebook page," Ben said. "I just got these babies a few days ago, so when I heard you were coming out for the event tonight, I knew I had to get you up here to play a few rounds."

Kleinberger laughed. "If we get bored with all the stiffs in suits downstairs, maybe we can sneak back up here and try out the Frogger game next."

"Deal." Ben cleared his throat. "Speaking of deals—"

"Yes, I suppose we should talk a bit more about the contracts." Kleinberger ran a hand over his snowy white hair, then straightened the lapels of his jacket. Like Ben, he wasn't wearing a tie, which Ben took as a good sign.

"There's no rush," Ben said. "You can take all the time

you need looking over the changes I proposed."

Kleinberger shook his head and gave a dry little chuckle. "Boy, you sure are different from your father. 'Take all the time you need.' You wouldn't believe how seldom I hear that in business these days."

Actually, Ben would believe it. He'd read an interview Kleinberger had done in *Forbes* magazine two years ago where the old man had expressed dismay at the rushed and thoughtless nature of modern business transactions. Never let it be said that CEO Ben Langley didn't pay attention.

You learned that from Holly. Among other things.

"I'm just glad I got to spend the afternoon with you, sir," Ben said. "I've really enjoyed learning more about how you and Mrs. Kleinberger built the company from the ground up."

"Please, call me Joe."

"Joe," Ben repeated. "Beyond all the negotiations and business dealings, it's been great getting to know you."

"Likewise. Maybe once all this business is settled, Margaret and I can have you out for dinner sometime."

"I'd like that," Ben said, meaning it. How many times had his dad closed a deal, then closed the door on any further personal relationships with the players involved? But that wasn't how Ben planned to run things. No way. Relationships mattered. They mattered a helluva lot, regardless of what they got you in the business world.

He'd learned that from Holly, too. He was still learning, even after a week of not seeing her.

The thought of Holly's absence made his gut twist a little, but he shook it off to give Kleinberger his full attention as the old man spoke again.

"The contracts look great," he was saying. "I'd like to spend a little more time with them if that's okay, but I'm really happy with some of the changes you've made. The whole team looked them over the other day and we're very impressed."

"Good. I'm glad." Ben cleared his throat. "I suppose we should get downstairs for the event."

"I suppose so." Kleinberger cast a longing look at Ben's collection of arcade games, and Ben made a mental note to slip the guy his office key later.

Then the old man turned and nodded to the door. "Go ahead, son. Lead the way."

The words echoed a little in Ben's mind, taking on a meaning well beyond what Joe Kleinberger had intended.

Lead the way.

For the first time in his life, Ben Langley was sure he knew how to do that.

"My pleasure," he said, and strode toward the door.

•••

Outside in the parking lot, Holly sat in her car staring through the windshield. Her gaze was focused on a smudge of bird poop above her left windshield wiper. How long had it been there? When was the last time she'd had her car cleaned?

You're stalling. And this is hardly the right train of thought for a professional woman getting ready to crash the event of the year to apologize to the man she loves.

At least she looked good. Miriam had seen to that. Holly glanced down and smoothed her hands over her dress, willing the butterflies to stop banging around against the walls of her stomach. She was decked out in a teal evening gown that Miriam insisted made her skin glow. The hemline skimmed her knees and she wore a pair of killer heels Miriam promised would accentuate her calves.

She wondered if Ben would notice.

Her mind drifted back to that blue silk dress and her first event with Ben. It seemed like a lifetime ago. She felt the pinprick of tears in her eyes, and she ordered herself to stop thinking about that.

The past wasn't the issue here. She was done letting old ghosts tell her how to run her life, watching them hover over her shoulder as they whispered words of doubt and deception in her ear.

Those spooky bastards could go to hell.

She was living for the present now. And the future—with Ben, if he'd have her.

What if he's not interested?

Holly shook her head to clear the negative thoughts. *You're a smart, savvy, career woman who just saved her own business. Now it's time to save something more important than that.*

She took a deep breath and pushed open the car door.

Chapter Fifteen

"And with that, I'd like to formally welcome the Kleinberger team to the Langley Enterprises family," Ben said, beaming with the smile Holly recognized as his most genuine. "We promise you've made the right choice. Thank you."

The ballroom erupted into applause, and Holly clapped from her spot behind a tall, potted palm tree. She'd tucked herself in the back of the room to remain unobtrusive, not wanting to embarrass Ben in his big moment, not wanting to rattle him before his speech.

But now she just felt like a stalker. A stalker wearing really uncomfortable shoes.

She moved forward as Ben began walking toward the edge of the stage. He'd nailed the speech. Most importantly, he'd done it without her. All that passion, all that energy, all that commanding presence had been up there on that stage with him, and he'd done it all on his own.

She edged toward the front of the room, hoping she could get to him before a crowd formed around the man of the hour. She wanted to tell him how proud she was, how well he'd handled himself up there on that stage.

But more importantly, she wanted to tell him she was sorry. That she wanted to be his partner, his helpmate, *his girlfriend*, if only he'd still have her.

She was nearing the front of the room now, and she resisted the urge to wipe her sweaty palms down the skirt of her beaded teal evening gown. A group of Kleinberger executives had clustered nearby, but as Ben stepped off the stage, she saw he was alone. She ordered herself not to run, not to fling herself into his arms the way she wanted to.

God, he was gorgeous. She watched him wave to a white-haired man who was slipping out the door, and her gaze locked on Ben's big, familiar palm. Then she let herself take in the rest of him, admiring the whole package. He wasn't wearing a tie or even a tux the way some of the other men were. But something about his presence made it clear this was a man in charge. This was a man who could roll up his shirtsleeves and get the job done. This was a man who didn't give a fuck about someone else's dress code.

"Ben," she said softly.

She thought her voice was too quiet to carry over the crowd, and she started to repeat herself.

But he must have heard her somehow. The instant his gaze swung to hers, a flood of warmth rushed through her body. She moved forward, her hands loose and awkward at her sides.

"Ben," she said again. She started to reach out and shake his hand, but stopped herself. Now wasn't the time to be businesslike Holly.

But with executives milling about on all sides of her, it wasn't the time to throw herself into his arms, either, so she settled for clasping her hands in front of her. "Congratulations," she said. "It was a beautiful speech. Truly amazing."

"Thank you." He looked her up and down, and she half

expected him to ask what the hell she was doing here. Instead, he smiled. "You look damn good," he said.

"Thank you. So do you." She took a shaky breath, her well-rehearsed speech fleeing her brain as she lost herself in those amber-flecked eyes. "Ben, I just wanted to say I'm sorry. I'm sorry and I'm proud of you and most of all, I miss you. I miss you *a lot*."

He opened his mouth to reply, but before he could say a word, Lyle Langley stepped up beside him and clapped his son on the shoulder. *Hard.*

"Ben, my boy! Nicely done. Of course, you could have added in a bit about the return-on-investment and skipped all that crap with the data about—"

"I'm sorry, Dad, could you give me a minute?" He gave his father a measured look. "I'm kind of in the middle of something."

Lyle looked at Holly and raised an eyebrow. Then he turned back to Ben. "I think you've got more pressing things to deal with right now."

"Actually, I don't." There was something intimidating in Ben's tone, something Holly had never heard before. "Nothing else is more important than the conversation I'm having right now."

"Ben." Lyle's voice was equally cold, and he glanced toward the team of Kleinberger execs making their way toward them. Lyle gave them a wave and a smile so sugary, Holly nearly choked on the saccharine. The Kleinberger team waved back, drawing closer now to their awkward little huddle.

Holly thought about trying to rescue Ben, but the steely look in his eye told her this was not a man who needed rescuing. This was a man who had everything under control.

Lyle looked at his son again. "Don't blow this. Now isn't the time to be making chit-chat with girls." Lyle turned to Holly and fired off another one of his schmoozy smiles. "Sweetheart, why don't you run over to the bar and grab us a couple glasses of Laphroig? The twenty-five-year, neat."

"That's enough, Dad!" Ben's voice carried over the crowd. Several people nearby stopped talking, and everyone turned to stare. The Kleinberger team froze, close enough now to hear every word of their conversation.

Ben stared at his dad. Lyle stared back.

Holly stared at them both and wondered if she should have come here at all.

Part of her expected Ben to back down. She'd hardly blame him if he did.

Instead, he reached for her hand. He pulled her close, slipping an arm around her waist as he nodded to the Kleinberger team one by one. "Holly, I'd like to introduce you to the Kleinberger executives. Gentlemen, this is Holly Colvin president of First Impressions PR and Branding."

"Hello," Holly said, conscious of Lyle simmering beside her. "It's a pleasure to meet you."

Ben ignored his father and focused on the introductions. "You've already met my father, of course," he said. "I'd like you to meet Carl, Jim, Harold, Gary, James, Floyd, Devon, and Jim."

"I've heard wonderful things about you," Holly said, shaking each man's hand in turn.

"I'll introduce you to Joe Kleinberger later," Ben said. "He's the company founder. Great guy. He had some business to take care of in my office, but he'll be back later."

A funny little knowing smile crossed Ben's face, but no one else seemed to notice. Holly nodded, conscious of Ben's arm around her waist. "I look forward to meeting him," she said.

"That's probably not necessary." Lyle Langley flashed another tooth-gritted smile and cupped a hand under Holly's elbow. "Say, sweetheart, could you run over there to the hors d'ouevres table and grab us a few—"

"Absolutely not!" Ben grabbed Lyle's hand and pried it off her elbow as he leveled his father with a look that could boil tar. "Holly's not here to do your bidding, Dad. She's not here to wait on you or serve as my arm candy or do anything other than be my companion and enjoy her evening."

Lyle frowned at Holly, then turned back to Ben and lowered his voice. "Son, I don't think you understand how these kinds of events usually go."

"Actually, I understand perfectly well. And I intend to change that. I intend to change a lot of things around here, as a matter of fact."

A few members of the Kleinberger team exchanged nervous glances. One man—Holly thought he was the CEO?—gave Ben a supportive nod. "We were actually very pleased with the alterations you proposed in the contract. The charitable component, the parts about giving back to the communities where you do business—all of that is very forward-thinking and totally in line with our corporate values."

"I'm glad," Ben said. "I studied your company's mission statement and met with Joe Kleinberger to make sure I had a good sense about the heart and soul of your business. The human element. What makes Kleinberger tick beyond the dollars and cents."

"This is absurd," Lyle muttered. "You can't just go changing contracts willy-nilly."

Ben turned back to his father. "Actually, Dad, I can—I'm in charge now." He pulled Holly tighter against him, giving her hand a reassuring squeeze. "And I'll be making a lot more changes around here. We're starting with how we treat, speak of, and address women. We're starting with the woman I love."

•••

Though Ben still had very little furniture in his penthouse suite, he had something much more important: the makings for ice cream floats.

The thought of sipping one was pure nirvana as Holly toed off her high heels and leaned against the granite bar while Ben got to work making their post-event treats.

"Is it wrong that I really enjoyed the look on your dad's face when you told him under no circumstances was he allowed to pat, squeeze, grab, or comment on any part of my body?" Holly asked.

"Or any woman's body," Ben pointed out as he scraped ice cream into the mixing cup. "Of course, yours is the body that interests me the most."

"I'm glad," she said, pushing her hair out of her face. "I'm sorry if I embarrassed you by showing up tonight."

"Are you kidding me? Seeing you there was the best part of my whole evening." He grinned. "Well, that and watching you and Joe Kleinberger go head-to-head at Space Invaders."

She laughed. "I enjoyed it, too."

"Good."

Holly bit her lip as she felt her smile start to wobble a little. She looked down at her hands, trying to regain her composure. When she looked up at him again, he was watching her with a curious expression. "Ben, I'm scared."

"Of my dad? Don't be, he's a prick, but I've got him handled."

"No, of these feelings. Of the fact that I'm so over-the-moon crazy about you and what that might mean for my future. For my career."

He smiled and stirred something into a tall glass. "Would it help if I promised you I'll never, ever, under any circumstances ask you to compromise your career for me?"

"Maybe?"

"And that I expect the same from you."

"Of course. I wouldn't have it any other way."

"It sounds like we're already off to a good start, then."

He plunked a tall, froth-filled glass in front of her. She hesitated, then hooked a finger around the old-fashioned red and white striped straw that looked like something from a retro soda shop. She wrapped her lips around it, conscious of Ben's eyes on her as she took her first sip.

"How is it?" he asked, leaning against the bar beside her and setting down his own glass.

"Delicious," she said, taking another sip. "But it's not a root beer float. What is it?"

"Yours is a lemon ginger float made with ginger beer and lemon sorbet. Mine is a classic PB & J float made with peanut butter ice cream and grape soda. Here, try some."

She did, savoring the delicious blend of sweet and nutty, savory and fruity. "It's good," she said. "They're both great."

Ben took a drink of hers and made a face, then grabbed his glass back. "I'm not a fan of yours, but this one's tasty." He scooped up a spoonful of ice cream, looking thoughtful. "And you know, that's okay."

"What's okay?"

"We can try different things or branch out in different directions without losing the core of ourselves or our belief in the other person. Hell, I can even decide I like Laphroiag."

"You're being philosophical about beverages now?"

"I am. This is my literary geek side. Did I mention I double-minored in philosophy and English?"

"You didn't."

"I am a man of many facets," he said, licking his spoon in a way Holly wished didn't make her think of what else he could do with his mouth. He caught her staring and grinned.

"Many facets," Holly repeated. "You don't say."

"So it's okay for us to experiment and try new things and let our tastes evolve and support each other through career changes and life transitions and all kinds of other bullshit. But you know what's not okay?"

"What?"

"Me being apart from you for even another day. I've missed you, Holly."

She swallowed hard, her throat clogging with emotion and lemon sorbet. "I've missed you, too." She nudged her glass aside, willing herself not to get choked up. "And I'm sorry, too. I'm sorry for not giving you the benefit of the doubt. For not trusting who you were at the core of it all. For thinking you could ever be like your father or like my ex-husband."

"It's okay. I'm sorry for not seeing earlier how scared you were and that I needed to do a better job showing you I had no intention of becoming a workaholic jerk like my father."

"You've shown me now," she said. "I believe you."

"I won't claim I won't have my jerky moments, but you're always free to call me on it. That's the way relationships work. We're both going to screw up every now and then."

He grinned and set his glass down, reaching for her hands. She looked down at them, feeling inexplicably happy at the sight of their intertwined fingers. When she met his gaze again, she smiled.

"So I'm sorry and you're sorry," she said.

"It looks that way."

"Okay, but who screwed up more?"

"What?"

She grinned. "I think we need to settle this fairly."

"Oh?"

"And I have an idea."

"Do tell."

She rearranged their fingers so their knuckles were interlocked, thumbs resting on top of their connected fists.

She met his eyes and felt her smile widen. "One, two, three, four, I declare a thumb war."

Ben smiled back and squeezed her hand tighter. "Five, six, seven, eight—Holly, I think you're really great." He leaned forward and kissed her. "In fact, I think I kinda love you."

Her stomach rolled over like a giddy puppy, and Holly fought the urge to crawl into his lap. "That doesn't rhyme," she said, kissing him back. "But I love you, too."

"Yeah?"

"Definitely."

"I'm glad."

She moved back, still eager to crawl all over him, but knowing it was more important now to reconnect on a different plane. "Okay then," she said, licking her lips. "Get ready to have your thumb's ass kicked."

Epilogue

"And that concludes today's presentation on the branding plan for the new philanthropic arm of Langley Enterprises. Does anyone have any questions?"

Holly pivoted at the front of the conference room to see Ben raising his hand. She smiled and pointed a manicured finger at him. "Yes, you there in front. What was your name again?"

"Benjamin Monroe Langley, but you can just call me your fiancé."

The word sent a bolt of pleasure coursing through her all over again, even though she'd had a month to get used to the idea of marrying Ben and three more since they first stripped off their clothes in this very conference room.

"Yes, Mr. Fiancé," she said, doing her best to maintain her business decorum even though they were the only two people in the room. "You had a question?"

"I did. I was wondering if you could tell me more about the penetrative testing involved with this product launch."

Holly grinned and folded her arms over her chest. "Well,

first we debriefed, then firmed up our action plan, and finally we had a robust interface."

Ben smiled and pushed his glasses up his nose. "I can get behind that."

She giggled and sat down beside him. "Seriously, what did you think? I know this is your pet project, and I want to make sure we do it justice."

"I think it's amazing," he said, leaning in for a kiss. "I especially love your proposal for Judy's Hope."

"I'm so glad. I wanted to incorporate your mother's legacy into it somehow, and it just made sense that the program funding cancer research should be named after her."

"She'd be very proud."

"She'd be very proud of you, Ben." She squeezed his hand. "Watching you evolve into the sort of CEO you were meant to be, instead of the CEO your father wanted you to be—I just wish she'd gotten to see it, too."

He smiled. "I think she'd be even more proud to see how wisely I've chosen her future daughter-in-law."

He leaned close, planting another kiss on her lips, and Holly slid her fingers into his hair to kiss him back hard and deep and sure.

"Okay, you two, put your clothes back on!" Miriam burst into the room with one hand covering her eyes, a look of mock disgust scrunching up her features. "Oh, who am I kidding? I kinda want to see Hottie McCEO in his undies."

"Nice effort, but no cigar," Ben said. "Better luck next time."

Miriam shrugged and dropped into a chair beside Ben. "Can't blame a girl for trying."

Holly sat down on the other side of Ben and kicked her shoes off. Ben reached down and pulled her feet into his lap. He wrapped his massive palms around the arch of one foot and began to massage her heel.

"Thank you, honey," she said, relaxing into her seat.

"My pleasure."

"I think I've almost got this Kleinberger presentation dialed in," Holly said, turning back to Miriam. "Do we have all the video footage finished?"

"We do, but that's not why I came in here. You know that meeting we scheduled for tomorrow afternoon?"

"The one with Urban Trax?"

"Yep. It's been cancelled."

"What's Urban Trax?" Ben asked.

"Only the second largest sporting goods retailer in the United States," Miriam said.

"And the fact that you haven't heard of them is exactly why they need our help rebranding," Holly added before turning back to Miriam. "So what's the problem?"

"They fired their CEO. I guess there was some sort of scandal. I didn't press for details."

"Oh no! So now what are they going to do?"

Miriam shrugged. "Sounds like they've already got a new CEO lined up and he wants to keep moving ahead. But he wants to meet with us first. Start over from ground zero, really assess where they're going."

"Ugh," Holly said, closing her eyes. "We're too swamped with other work to pile more on our plates. Do you think we should hire someone else to help restart the process?"

"I might have the bandwidth," Miriam said. "I just handed off the Jamboree Jams account to Sarah, so I have an unexpected opening in my schedule."

"You?" Ben said. "In charge of a sporting goods store?" He grinned and squeezed Holly's foot. "This should be interesting."

Miriam rolled her eyes. "What's that supposed to mean, Smarty McSnootypants?"

"Just that you're the last person in the world I could ever

imagine working with a client like that. Your idea of outdoorsy is walking from the car to the nail salon."

Holly laughed, secretly delighted by the teasing that always erupted between Ben and her best friend. "And your idea of roughing it is having to wait two weeks between pedicure appointments," she chimed in. "Or missing your morning espresso from Starbucks."

"And her favorite form of exercise is running—*her charge card*!"

"Yeah, yeah," Miriam said, waving a dismissive hand. "And the last time I went hiking was when the escalator broke at Barney's. I've heard it. I still think I can handle the account."

"Oh, I don't doubt you can handle it," Holly said. "My question is whether they can handle you?"

Miriam grinned and folded her arms over her chest. "I certainly hope so."

Acknowledgments

Thanks so much to my brilliant and beautiful critique partners and beta readers, Cynthia Reese, Linda Grimes, Larie Borden, Bridget McGinn, and Minta Powelson. You never cease to amaze me with your insightful commentary and your willingness to read my early draft drivel.

As always, I'm hugely grateful for my agent, Michelle Wolfson. Thanks for sticking with me through thick and thin and making this whole publishing thing both bearable and fun. Looks like our train is finally rolling, huh?

Endless thanks to the whole Entangled team, including Heather Howland, Stephen Morgan, Liz Pelletier, Debbie Suzuki, Jessica Turner, Melanie Smith, Heather Riccio, Crystal Havens, Julia Knapman, and anyone else I may have omitted but am nonetheless indebted to for your tireless work and endless talent. I also tip my hat to Danielle Sanchez and the rest of the crew at Inkslinger PR.

Oodles of gratitude to all my Facebook pals who came through for me with delightfully filthy business jargon. Much love and thanks to Lorainne Hollister, Trisha Leigh

Zieghorn, Bayley Shirley, Lori Robinett, Peter Koevari, Laura Bickle, Dawn Metcalf, Meg West, Beth Merlott Reinker, Deb Ofstedal, Elizabeth E. Neal, Jenna McCarthy, Pat O'Rourke, Monica Stecher, Judah McAuley, Sally Schrumph, Jessica Lemmon, Hank Therien, Bri Brey, Terri Lynn Coop, David Spillet, CeliaSue Hecht, Kellie Flanagan, Paul Henry, Laura Crawford, Jeff Taylor, Kim Garrity Geer, Ann Marie Patterson, Justin Farmer, Marcy Whittington Meyer, Jane Wu, Kari Lynn Dell, Kim Rossi Stagliano, Phil Hall, Gina Todaro Freed, Vince Gordon, Aric Bright, Scott Caputo, Hanna St. John, Glen Gerrard Thuncher, Ryan Ositis, and James Justt.

I'm so very thankful for the love and support of my family, Dixie and David Fenske, Aaron and Carlie Fenske, and my awesome stepkids, Cedar and Violet. I'm so lucky to have all of you.

And thank you to Craig for being the sexiest geek I know (and a damn fine husband to boot). Love you, baby!

About the Author

Tawna Fenske traveled a career path that took her from newspaper reporter to English teacher in Venezuela to marketing geek to PR manager for her city's tourism bureau. An avid globetrotter and social media fiend, Tawna is the author of the popular blog, Don't Pet Me, I'm Writing, and a member of Romance Writers of America. She lives with her husband in Bend, Oregon, where she'll invent any excuse to hike, bike, snowshoe, float the river, or sip wine on her back deck. She's published several romantic comedies with Sourcebooks, including Making Waves, which was nominated for contemporary romance of the year by RT Book Reviews. She also writes heartwarming series books for Entangled Publishing, and tender, funny romances for Montlake Publishing. Tawna's quirky brand of comedy and romance has won praises from Kirkus Reviews, which noted, "Up-and-coming romance author Fenske sets up impeccable internal and external conflict and sizzling sexual tension for a poignant love story between two engaging characters, then infuses it with witty dialogue and lively humor. An appealing blend of lighthearted fun and emotional tenderness."

9 781682 810569